The Myth of Midget Molley:

King of the Boardwalk

By Ali Rob

D-Bear Publications   **Ali Rob**

Copyright ©2006 by D-Bear Publications

All rights reserved. No part of this book may be reproduced or transmitted in any form or by any means, electronic or mechanical, including photocopying, recording, or by any information storage and retrieval system without the written permission from the publisher or author except for the inclusion of brief quotations in a review.

This is a work of fiction. It is not meant to depict, portray or represent any real persons. All the characters, incidents and dialogues are the products of the author's imagination and are not to be construed as real. Any resemblance to events or persons, living or dead, is purely coincidental.

First Printing November 2006.

ISBN: 0-9790048-4-5
       978-0-9790048-4-1

WELCOME TO D-BEAR PUBLICATIONS
&
D-BEAR ENTERTAINMENT

Thank you for choosing D-Bear's premier title, "The Myth of Midget Molley: Life and Love of Kingpin," by Ali Rob. We value your business and invite you to enter a relationship with.

The D-Bear brand comprises two companines, D-Bear Pulblications and D-Bear Enterainment. Both are forged with the hope that those who engage us will not only be entertained, but also enlightened.

Please visit www.midgetmolley.com and feel free to send us an email, check us out at myspace, or give out us shout.

DBEAR_PUBLICATIONS@yahoo.com
xx7midget_the_kingpin7xx@yahoo.com
www.myspace.com/midgetmolley
www.myspace.com/abdulshaheed

D-Bear is always seeking out new relevant material to publish. Interested authors should submit manuscripts double-spaced in MS Word format via email or mail hard copies to:

D-Bear Publications
P.O. Box 8044
Atlantic City, NJ 08404
(609)-289-8894

D-Bear Publications   Ali Rob

Greetings to:

Mrs Elise Molley, Haneef Molley & The Molley Mob, Katrina Wilson, Hakeem Vaughn, Hakeema Vaughn & The Vaughn Family, Kenyetta & Vanessa Anderson, Josephine & AbdulShaheed Cunningham, Adrienne & Chanel Aisha Shaheed, Lisa & Trinity Demps, Lorena Reed, Matt "Muz" Bell, Lucy Breton, Gloria & Angel Diaz, THE BROTHERHOOD: Sekou "Shaykh" Odinga, Jeff "Malik" Fort, Donte "Sharif" Brown, Reggie "Saboor" Nelson, Stephan "Basil" Richards, Jerome "Mujahid" Williams, Domnick "Raha" Batts, Kendall "Muhammad" Smith, Mack "Qaddim" Triston, Lealon "Amir" Muldrow, Darrius Abullah, Eddie "Rahman" Jennings. Alonzo "Baba" Jerrell, Freddie "Mubeen" Taylor, Kevin Jackson, Cecil "Hanif" Allen. H.A. Shaheed. Stanley "Abdul-Mumin Muhajir" Cummings, WillPam "Ali" Clark, Dwayne "Mujahid" McDonald, Anthony "Wail" Austin, Shaheed Omar; Friends: Angel Mitchell, Jamie and George Rex, April Valentine, Sherema Copes, Llyod and Sharon Dogget, Joe and Charlene Fleming, Shawn and Erika Zauzig, Josh & Gayle Mansuy, Tara, Judy Yuri, Steve, Big Amp, Volaunta Connor, Katherine "Kitten" King, Lacy Bernadette, Philly Carol, Faheem, Steve Young, William "Speedy" Marsh, Rodney Jerkins & The Dark Child Family, Bill Sawyer, Doug Wiggins, Earl Borne Harris,

The Myth of Midget Molley   **Ali Rob**

Ray-Ray Rosario, Joe Margolis, Ronnie McKinley, Bruce, Troy & Kevin Hamlet, Gwen & Lewis Todd. Delora, Norma, Pappy Mason, Tiger June-Boy, (Outlaw) David McGraw, Pauline "Ameenah" Phillips, My nieces, My Nephews & all my cousins – the Gayles, Dabneys, Molleys, Allens, Simmons, Caesars, Manfields, McKinleys Nelsons, Curtis' & Plummers'. If I forgot Anyone, charge it to my head and not my heart.

Special Thanks To:
Kevin Jackson & Jackson Press

...Missing You

Mrs. Helen L. Molley, Jeanie "Khalilah" Molley, Mrs Denise Molley, Catherine Dabney, Mrs. Ruth Vaughn, Michael "D Bear" Demps, Lamont "lil Ump" Wilson, Tyree "Ty" White, Marshall "Musa" Jones, Zebedee "Aziz" Newmones, Tyrone Williams, Leavander Johnson, Robert "Robby" Hart, Richard "Mustafa" Kirkland, Jerome "Ali" Miller and To all who died in a senseless drug war, Rest In Peace.

Mortui Vivis Praecipant
(Let the dead teach the living)

D-Bear Publications   Ali Rob

FORWARD

By Ali Rob and Midget Molley

When I sat down to write the forward to THE MYTH OF MIDGET MOLLEY, I didn't know where to begin. I contacted Hakeem Abdul Shaheed a.k.a. Midget Molley at the super maximum federal penitentiary in Marion, Illinois. Since it was his story, I knew he was the perfect one to introduce his story. He never responded to my letters. I even tried visiting and he refused me.

On October 3, 2006, five years after my initial contact with Mr. Molley, his circumstance took a harsh turn. I received from his wife, Elise, that Midget was brutally tortured by the guards in Marion after a minor incident. Internal Affairs ordered his immediate transfer to the federal penitentiary in Terre Haute, Indiana where he was placed on death row. Out of concern, I wrote Mr. Molley a letter asking if there was anything I could do for him. The candor of his response shocked me. Where my story spins the tale of his lavish life as a kingpin 20 years ago, he informs of the unexpected brutal aftermath which still persists 20 years later. **Read his forward below...**

Crack came...All morals and manners faded away. Money and murder were the orders of the day. Unlike

The Myth of Midget Molley   Ali Rob

the 60's and 70's when hustlers did their best to shield the youth from the life they lived, crack dealers targeted the youth as runners, touters, and in some cases, cold-blooded killers.

Though its been nearly 20-years since I been sentenced, I can still hear the words of Judge Joseph Rodriguez when he passed sentence on me:

> You have destroyed the community; You have spread death and destruction in your own community, I cannot see sentencing you less than 300-months, 25-years. You have hurt more people than you have helped. Many lives have been lost and ruined because of your actions. Your apparent remorse can not bring back the lives of those who are dead. 20-years to serve and 5-years supervised release is the appropriate sentence for you. You destroyed so many people.

At the time Judge Rodriguez uttered those words, I could not understand what he meant when he said I caused the death of others. But I've had plenty of time to think since my sentencing.

As I look back, I see the 80's crack-era as a very violent time. In 1988, there were 500-murders in Washington D.C. alone. Bodies were dropping every day. No one cared because the law-abiding people basically wrote us off as animals. IT WAS KILL OR BE KILLED. The money was so plentiful, most of us gambled our lives against making fast loot.

Those who were smart, some would say blessed,

came out of that era with their lives. My friends Robert "Robby" Hart (from A.C.) and Walter Harrell (from D.C.) both lost their lives to the crack game. Of course there was Jesse Rice, who many thought I killed, murdered at the tender age of seventeen. All these senseless deaths came about because of the unstructured nature of the crack game. The 60's and 70's produced hustlers. The 80's produced misguided drug dealers, blinded by the free fall of money that seemed to float down from heaven.

I, Midget Molley, am here to write this forward because, although I helped a few people prosper with the millions of dollars that crack cocaine produced for me, I now understand the judgment levied against me at my sentencing...

***Author's note: Mr. Molley was released from death row on June 14, 2006 by order of the United States Department of Justice. Investigators had reviewed surveillance tapes from the incident and found Midget was violated by several guards. Nine were removed from duty at Marion and now face criminal charges for violating the civil rights of Hakeem Shaheed a.k.a. Midget Molley and Tyrone "Sayfullah" Davis, a fellow Muslim.

Chapter 1
DAMN!

We interrupt this program to bring you an ACTION NEWS special report:

"Federal Agents have arrested the notorious drug kingpin Midget Molley, leader of the murderous ASO Posse, along with his personal bodyguard Tyree Jenkins and his mistress Rosetta B. Divine, as they drove across the Delaware Memorial Bridge.

Authorities say Mr. Molley, who often flaunted his drug financed wealth by wearing a gold crown, was the sole leader of a multi-kilo cocaine distribution network that garnered $1,000,000 a month in the Atlantic City public housing projects.

Stay tuned on ACTION NEWS for full details of the arrest at 5pm." (February 14, 1989)

Midget Molley's madness began in February 1975 when his spiritual leader, the Honorable Elijah Muhammad, passed away. Temple #10, like the other eighty or so temples around the country, erupted in a sort of cult-like scream of disbelief and shock at the news of his death. For nearly fifty years, the diminutive leader of the Nation of Islam indoctrinated his followers with a message of black supremacy and white inferiority, telling them that he was the Messenger of God sent to them. After him, Muhammad taught, there'd be no other "Messenger" t come until another twenty-five thousand years. He taught them that the white man was the devil and the black man was god the king, the ruler, the master of the earth.

    Brother 8X, the name Midget was known by in Temple #10, believed like most of his fellow members, that Elijah Muhammad was invincible, that he couldn't die. So when the news of his death came to them on that cold, rainy day he joined in that horrifying chorus of disbelief. Midget had been a part of the Nation since he was 14-years old. Now he was among half-a-million followers who'd lost their leader, teacher and guide. After years of being told when to eat, sleep, stand, sit and speak, they were now left alone like a ship lost at sea with no captain, no rudder, or no navigational equipment to make it through the tumultuous storm that'd engulfed them. Some committed suicide. Some joined the church. Others returned to a life of drug-abuse, prostitution and other criminal activities.

    Back in 1975, there were no casinos. Atlantic City, once a grand East coast tourist Mecca, had become a wasteland, a cesspool of poverty. From 1920 to 1960 the city were boomed. But since then, the town slowly deteriorated into nothing more than bars and churches on each corner desperately competing for the minds and welfare checks of the poor. The Nation of Islam had

The Myth of Midget Molley   Ali Rob

been the only bright light among all this blight until it too flickered, dimmed and died.

Now left to sort out his own survival, Midget chose a street life of selling heroin. That is until he was sent to jail for manslaughter in 1980 for killing Brian Collins. Brian and his Back Maryland Crew were on some clean up the community shit, supposedly to rid the hood of drugs and violence. But Midget knew better. He knew they were no more than a crew of disgruntled drug dealers posing to clear the territory in order to set up their operation. The BMC's tactics were brutal. Already they'd kidnapped and killed Anthony B. And they'd left two members of the A-Team for dead. Midget had many loyal contacts in the streets and word quickly made it back to him that the BMC Boys were coming for him too. He knew then he had no choice but to leave town or act first. Never being one to run from a fight, Midget chose the later.

"Fuck those Motherfuckers," Midget said to himself. "My kids gotta eat."

Midget held to that thought, waiting for the right moment to strike. The right time came on a cold New Jersey night. As he stood on the Strip in front of the Red Klox Bar, Midget felt the winter air reach all the way to the bottom of his lungs.

"*Of all nights to be out here slinging, it had to be this one*" Midget thought to himself. "Fuck this shit, I'm going home."

As he moved towards his dark blue Park Avenue,

one of his girls, Kim Mickens ran up on him. The long-legged chinky-eyed beauty fast became his favorite by proving herself resourceful in the streets and quite freaky in the bed.

"Yo Kim, what's up!?" Midget asked "You alright!?"

"No! I just saw Brian and 'em Back Maryland! They in the parking lot! C'mon! Hurry up! They should still be there!"

Back Maryland was about five blocks from Red Klox Bar. Midget knew this was his time.

"Here. Drive." he said tossing her the keys.

Kim caught the keys and ran to the driver's side. As she cranked the engine and threw it in drive, Midget prepared to kill. By the time they'd reached the end of the one-mile stretch, Midget's demeanor had changed. Brian was no longer human, but a cold-blooded animal who had to be killed.

"Park over there," Midget directed Kim.

Midget checked his .45 semi-automatic. In one quick step he pulled back on the bolt, moving a round the chamber.

Kim, turned on by the danger of it all, leaned over and kissed him passionately with her sexy-thin lips.

"Be careful," she said reclining back in the seat. "I don't know what I'll do without that good dick."

As Midget moved forward he plotted his approach. There was an opening between the apartments that made the walk-through resemble an alley. Midget chose to move through that dark, narrow passageway. He

The Myth of Midget Molley   Ali Rob

could hear Brian and his crew chattering with laughter in the distance. Ahead in the distance, there they stood. Midget bit down hard, grinding his teeth together. His hands sweated. His heart pounded. His eyes burned with fanatical fire. He was hot with anticipation. Finally his moment arrived. There was no turning back — Brian, Maurice, James and the Turner twins resembled sitting ducks as they stood posted up against the wall smoking weed.

"Yeah motha fucka! You lookin for me?!" **Boom! Boom!! Boom!!!**

Midget squeezed off every round, causing the big gun to almost bust out of his little hand. Before Brian knew what had hit him he was dead. Midget quickly ran from the murder scene with an angry satisfaction that his point had been made, *"Don't fuck with me! And don't fuck with my family!"*

Throughout his prison bid, the image of Brian's lifeless body falling to the ground remained vivid in Midget's mind. He could still hear the frightening screams of friends and see the globs of blood pumping from Brian's head as if it had all happened yesterday. But it had been five long-years of incarceration and it was time for Midget to go home.

"Molley, Let's go," said the prison guard, "It's time to pack up."

"Ok," said Midget from his Rahway State Prison cell, "I'm ready."

Midget grabbed the box he'd packed the night before

and left his narrow cell. After going through about 30 minutes of paperwork, Midget was now free.

"Good luck, Mr. Molley," said Sergeant Miller.

"Bitch! You need the luck," Midget thought to himself. "I got Allah."

Moving from confinement the main prison lobby, Midget scanned the room until he peeped out Myeesha. There she was, standing about 10 feet away smiling that Chucky-Cheese smile of hers. Excited to be able to touch her husband, Myeesha flew into Midget's arms, wrapping her warm, petite anatomy around the man she'd waited for so faithfully. The same old, beat-up Monte Carlo Myeesha used to drive to visit him in prison waited in the parking lot. Tyeesha, his wife's identical twin sister, excitedly struggled to get the car door open.

"Reach through the window and open it from the outside," Myeesha yelled.

Midget smiled and took a deep breath of the warm summer morning breeze as he turned and looked back at the huge concrete structure that held him captive for so many years. From the outside looking in no one could ever know the pain of prison life without living it. It was a pain of isolation and disconnection, of no mail, no money, or mercy.

To Midget Rahway had been a four-walled hell. He'd seen the most violent acts committed over matters as arbitrary as a place in line or a cigarette. Rahway had been a pit filled with hateful men preying on the vulnerability of the weak, the meek and the misguided, a place where frequent midnight screams snatched the strongest of men from their sleep. Those screams were from a kid getting raped by a man who'd himself been molested. This was Midget's reality for sixty months, a reality he wanted to just forget.

After taking another deep breath of freedom, he sat in the backseat of the hot Monte Carlo.

"Look at you!" Tyeesha shouted with joy turning around, placing her small hands around his huge biceps. "You got so big. Let's get away from here before they find another reason to lock you up."

Myeesha pulled out of the prison parking-lot and drove the loud-motored car onto the New Jersey Turnpike as it backfired, scaring the shit out of Midget. Atlantic City was two hours from Rahway. The signs on the Turnpike caused his mind to instantly flashback to his prison time.

"WORK CALL! WORK CALL!" blared through the intercom.

The cell door rattled as it was electronically opened. He recalled the Hundreds of men who wouldn't think about going to work on the streets, happily leaving from their cages for the steel shop to press out the very highway signs Myeesha was speeding by on the New Jersey Turnpike. Despite the hardship of prison life, nothing in Rahway allowed Midget to forget that little big city by the sea. In his cell, he posted countless pictures. In his heart he stored indelible memories. Ironically, his job in the steel shop brought him the closest. He was responsible for making many of the street signs that marked Atlantic City. Going to work became his personal Monopoly game.

Many from outside Atlantic City don't know that the Monopoly game was designed to reflect the streetnames in Atlantic City, just as they don't know that the City is actually an Island, like Manhattan, surrounded by the Atlantic Ocean and the Back Bay. No banks are ever robbed because there're only three ways in and three ways out: the Black Horse Pike, the White Horse Pike and the Atlantic City Expressway. Once these three arteries are cut-off, you're trapped.

"What's up?" Tyeesha excitedly asked, as she turned aga look at her brother-in-law. "You ain't talkin'. What 's up?"

Midget tried to force a smile on his face but his thoughts wouldn't allow it.

"Ain't nothin," he blurted. "Same ole shit."

His mind was still in shock from the scarring psychological effects of prison life. Just that very morning, an 18-year old kid from Newark had been found hanged in his cell. Prisoners passed by as if he was a slab of meat hanging on a hook at some slaughter-house. His name was Young Black and no sympathy, sadness, or shame was shown. He'd been convicted of double-involuntary manslaughter and sentenced to three years for selling crack to a pregnant woman. The 18-year-old addict took a lethal dose, leading not only to her death,

The Myth of Midget Molley   Ali Rob

but also the death of her unborn fetus. Word on the Yard had it that he'd been strangled by an old convict, also from Newark, who'd been in for 15 years for bank robbery.

Those who've never been there will never understand the horror that exists behind the walls where America hides her shame. Tyeesha was clueless.

"Do guys really get raped in prison?" she asked. "Have you ever fucked a..."

"Tyeesha!" her sister shouted, as the car swerved left and right.

Midget laughed out loud loudly for the first time in five years.

He and Tyeesha had always been very close. She was the outspoken and outgoing of the twins.

"No," he said. "I never fucked anything in jail: no girls, no guards, no guys, no nothin'."

Myeesha sensed he was being sarcastic. Rolling her eyes, she kept driving. She recalled that visit where Midget had wanted her to have sex with him in the visiting room and she'd refused. They got into a big argument and Midget had become so steamed, he had to be forcibly removed from the visiting hall. He wound up in administrative segregation, or Ad Seg, for a week over that incident.

Finally, the beat up but ever reliable Monte Carlo pulled into the suburban town of Pleasantville. Today it's called Killville. Back when Midget was on the scene they called it P'ville. It was a quiet town six miles outside of Atlantic City where black people who made a little money, whether through hard work or hustle, bought their homes.

"Who live here?" Midget asked.

"My mother," said Myeesha.

"Wow, Y'all sure come a long way from Bacharach," he said, talking about the apartment complex on Bacharach Boulevard where Myeesha and her family first started out in after moving from Newark.

"No," she said. "My mom's come a long way. I still stay in the apartment you rented for me and the children, and this is your mother's car. I told you that the Park Avenue got repossessed back in '81 and that your brother crashed the Lincoln, but the only thing that was on your mind was sex."

"Don't you two start arguing already," Tyeesha pleaded.

But Midget, already silenced by his guilt, felt no need to argue. The pain he saw in his wife's eyes said it all.

As he climbed out of the backseat, he followed the twins up the few steps leading to a spacious porch. Guilt quickly became lust as the sight of Myeesha in pink shorts arrested his attention. Her butt was big and it methodically bounced with each step she took. She had an ass he didn't mind being locked up in. For five years the closest things he'd had to his wife were negligee photos and warm memories of how good her sex had been. His right-hand became his constant compan-

The Myth of Midget Molley   Ali Rob

ion through the years.

Now he was home, eyeing those shorts that hugged Myeesha's ass with possessive authority. His heart sped with horniness as she bent-over to pick up some toys left on the steps.

"I told these damn kids about leaving their toys out here," she complained.

Myeesha was beautiful, even when angry, thought Midget. And God was so gracious as to grant this one City with a reflection of her beauty. Her caramel-colored complexion was as sweet to the eyes as candy is to the mouth. The twins both stood about 5' 5" and weighed 125-pounds. Their shoulder length hair was jet black and silky-smooth, a perfect match for their sable eyes.

In a chair on the porch sat Grandma Ruby, the twins' grandmother. She was a picture of grace; as dark as the African nights with long, lustrous hair, high Cherokee cheek bones and pearly white teeth.

"Lord Jesus," she exclaimed. "Boy, give granny a hug."

Midget fell into her elderly embrace, feeling welcomed to be home. She was the only grandmother he'd ever known. His maternal and paternal grandparents had all passed before he was born.

The screen door flew open and out ran Hyleem, Midget's first-born.

"Daddy! Daddy!" he shouted, wrapping his arms around his father's shoulders.

The last time he saw his son he was eight years old.

Now he was about to be thirteen and taller than his father.

"Salaama' laykum," said Midget.

"Hyleemah is in the house hidin' behind the couch," said his son.

"Did you just hear me?" asked Midget.

"Oh. Wa'laykum Salaam, daddy."

Inside the house, six-year-old Hyleemah was hiding exactly where her brother said.

"Boo!" she shouted with laughter, jumping from behind the sofa.

"Hi baby; How's daddy's little girl?" he asked, lifting her in the air and kissing her.

"Hyleem be hittin' me and..."

"No I don't," Hyleem interrupted.

"Yes he do," she complained.

Midget felt happy just to hear his children's voices and see them giggling as they chased each other. In prison, the laughter had been hollow and most conversations were shallow. Midget had had to be very careful because a smile could be used to disarm for manipulation.

"Hi, ugly," said Ms. Rena, Myeesha's mother as she walked into the living-room from the kitchen, "welcome home."

It was his mother-in-law who'd given her daughter the emotional strength and spiritual encouragement to stand by Midget during his incarceration.

"Look at you," she said. "Look like you grew a few

The Myth of Midget Molley   Ali Rob

inches and finally gained some weight."

When Midget entered prison, he stood only five-three and weighed a hundred and twenty pounds. Now he was weighing 165 lbs and standing five feet, five inches. But everyone knew his true height and weight came from his heart.

"Yes Ma'am," he agreed. "I gained a little and grew a couple of inches."

"You hungry?" Ms. Rena asked.

"No, ma'am, I'm not hungry," Midget said. "I just wanna see my mom."

"Myeesha," she demanded, "take this boy to see his mother."

The Hatchet family had been up North since 1969, but their mannerisms and hospitality had remained Southern. They were generous, honest and loyal to a fault.

"What's all this noise down here?" a voice from upstairs asked.

It was Yolanda, one of Myeesha's four sisters.

"Hi Stranger," spoke Midget.

"Oh my God!" she said with a tone of disbelief. "Look at you."

She walked over to him and draped her long arms over his shoulders, measuring him with her almond eyes.

"I can't believe this, You finally made it home."

Chapter 2
BIG LOU CALLED

Midget stood in his mother-in-law's living room. He smiled as he observed the wedding pictures. His chocolate complexion and affectionate smile hadn't changed much since meeting Myeesha Hatchet. They'd been together all this time. They married when he was twenty-one. By 23, Midget was behind bars. Now, almost 29, he had nothing to show for it. What little money he used to have, he'd paid to his high-priced attorney, Pete Bruno. All he had left was a stressed out wife and two children. All his former street-corner partners were either hooked on drugs, in prison, or dead. Midget knew he had to come up, but how?

Myeesha and her mother, Ms. Rena walked back in the room.

"Baby, everything will be alright," Ms. Rena sad, placing her hands on his cheeks.

Midget knew she didn't want him returning to the streets and he was going to do everything he could to stay clean.

"Do you and your brother want to go with us?" asked Myeesha.

"Where?" Hyleemah asked.

"Over your Grandma Helen's house."

"I wanna go," said Hyleem.

The Myth of Midget Molley   Ali Rob

"Me too," pleaded Hyleemah.

"Well stop running around in here like you're outside," Myeesha ordered.

"Hyleem keep chasing me," said Hyleemah

"See," she said. "this is what I had to put up with while you were in prison; they're so damn terrible."

"No we not daddy," said Hyleemah running to the other side of the sofa to catch her breath. "Mommy just stressed out."

"How you know?" asked Midget bursting into laughter.

"Cause that's what Aunt Tyeesha and Grandma Rena be sayin'."

"Just get in the damn car," Myeesha demanded.

Midget could see what was really going on. After five long years, Myeesha was sexually frustrated.

The family made its way down Artic Avenue with Myeesha driving.

"Slow down, honey," said Midget excited to be on his old stomping grounds. "Ain't that June-Bug right there?"

"Where?" Myeesha asked.

"Right there," he said pointing as they crossed over Indiana Avenue.

"God he look bad," she said. "There go Seymour."

Midget just looked at him.

Seymour Jones was a stick-up kid who hated everything about Midget. They knew each other through Midget's brother Yunus. They used to be cool but one night when he was drunk outside of a club, Seymour called Midget a fake-ass nigga. Seymour was just joking, but Midget was quick tempered and shot him, leaving him with a permanent limp.

Midget would have killed him had Yunus been elsewhere.

"Stop right here," Midget yelled. "Pull on Gino's parking-lot!"

Excitedly, he jumped out and ran across Kentucky and Artic. They used to call it K-Y and the Curb, the heart and soul of black Atlantic City, the original Strip. Midget recalled how Duke Ellington, the Delphonics, Billie Holiday and Billy Paul all used to stand right at that corner after their gigs. The Strip had two main clubs, the Wonder Garden and Club Harlem.

As a youth, he used to spend his summers shining shoes on the strip. That's when he got his first taste of the street life.

Gangatas from Philadelphia and New York used to come through to catch a show and to stroll along the Boardwalk. Their presence overwhelmed young shoeshine kids like Midget.

Only 12-years-old at the time, he shined the shoes of many of these Black Gangstas like Mr. Palmer, Mr. Williams, Georgia Pete, Black Sam and Bo Diddles.

Observing the respect they got from the local gangstas, Midget had his first rush for the streets.

As he walked the Strip, an old wheelchair-bound man caught his attention. It was his old mentor, Mr.

The Myth of Midget Molley   Ali Rob

Kirkland.

"Hey there Pop," said Midget with exaggerated bass in his voice.

The old blind man swigged his wine and licked his lips with a smile.

"He know it's you," whispered Kenny an old worker who came up when he saw Midget.

"Hey, old head," Midget joked again.

The old man sat his wine bottle down.

"Little Caesar," he shouted, extending his arms to hug Midget. "You made it son, you made it."

Midget's eyes were teary.

"Come on, give me a hug," said Mr. Kirkland. "When you get out?"

"Just got out today."

"It feels good to hug you Caesar."

"It feels good to hug you too Pops."

Midget had confided in the old man when the BMC Boys were plotting on his life and now was getting his advice again.

"It's a new world out here Caesar," said Mr. Kirkland.

"That's what I'd heard on the yard."

"Where's Kenny?"

"He ran to the other side of the Street with everyone else."

"I'm sure they're all glad to see you.

"I'm glad to be seen," said Midget.

"The game's changed Caesar."

"I can handle it."

"Well, you come talk to me before you do anything," directed the old man. "You hear me son?"

"Yeah Pops," said Midget. "I'll be back through to see you soon."

Midget kissed his Pops on the forehead and ran back to the car.

Pops, or Mr. Kirkland, was an original gangster from the 1950s. He gave Midget the street-name "Little Caesar" back in late 1975 when he showed up on the strip sporting a sky-blue polyester suit, a rabbit-coat and a rabbit-hat. He gave away free quarters of hero every addict who came up to him that day. Every morning after that, he had his crew distributed free dime bags as a wake up shot.

As Midget moved towards the car and Myeesha, he embraced old clientele.

In the distance a young buck, Peanut, hopped on top of the mailbox.

"He think he's gonna get back out here and do the same thing."

"He washed up," said Junior.

Both were no more than 15-years-old. Unlike Midget, these kids were ruthless. Old addicts were afraid to speak up like they used to in the 70's. If addicts complained about quality, the new jacks fucked them up. The two looked like kids, but their innocence had long since left. The whole game had changed.

"Call Billy over here," said Peanut.

The Myth of Midget Molley　　　　　　　　Ali Rob

"Hey Billy," Junior yelled out to the addict. "Come here."

Billy dragged his worn body over.

"What was Midget talkin' 'bout?" inquired Peanut.

Billy pulled at his disheveled beard and remained silent. Frustrated, Peanut slapped him upside the head.

"What was Midget talkin' 'bout!?" Peanut barked.

"Nothin'," replied Billy

Junior pulled his gun and jammed it up Billy's chin.

"What was he sayin!" he growled.

"Yo! what the fuck y'all doin?!" Tone shouted out from across the street. "Go 'head leave Billy."

The pair turned from Billy and ran over to old man Kirkland. They laughed at the one-time gangsta of K-Y and the Curb, taunting him by running his wheelchair in between moving cars.

The soft voice spoke gently from the intercom.

"Who is it?"

"It's me Mrs. Helen, Myeesha."

Midget's mother buzzed them through door.

"You have to sign the log-book," said the well-kept security guard.

Midget looked around in amazement. The Emmit Till Towers was one of many complexes built while he was in prison.

After signing, they moved to the elevator.

"Let me push it," shouted Hyleemah.

"Shhh..." Myeesha cautioned. "Go ahead, Press it."
"I wanted to push it," Hyleem said.
"She pressed the button the last time."
Myeesha looked at Midget as if to say, "here we go."
The elevator glided up to the tenth floor. A serene bell chimed and the doors opened. Hyleem and Hyleemah ran off in hot pursuit.
"They your children," his wife smiled, kissing him on the face as they walked out of the elevator.
"Is that you Myeesha?" Mrs. Helen asked.
"Yes."
Helen opened the door and there he was.
"I love you mom," said Midget.
Caught of guard Mrs. Helen turned around.
"Oh, Jesus! Praise his name," she declared with tears now streaming.
That was the first time Midget had ever seen his mother cry. Struck by her emotions, he vowed to leave the streets alone even though deep down he knew this was impossible.
"Jesus loves you," his mother said through the tears.
Her honey-brown, round-face was soft and angelic. Midget pushed her tears away with his thumbs and wrapped her in his arms.
"Lord Jesus," she whispered as her head rested on his chest.
Midget didn't understand his mother's devotion to Jesus.

The Myth of Midget Molley   Ali Rob

"*Where was Jesus when you needed him?*" Midget angrily thought to himself. "*Where is he now? You're driving an old beat up car back and forth to the dialysis unit three days a week for life-saving treatments and...*"

"You hungry?" his mother asked, rescuing him from those thoughts.

"Yes."

"What do you want?"

"Some fried-chicken and potato-salad," he said with a smile.

"I already have some cooked," she said. "Your brother said he was coming over but never came."

"Which one?"

"Art."

"Have you heard from Yunus?"

"He called last week and said he'll be home soon."

"He only had a parole violation, right?"

"I don't know, I asked Jesus to look after him."

Midget sighed to himself as he sat down to eat. He saw organized religion as a mass sedative for the poor.

He believed in God but felt God gave His people freedom to choose how they believed. Midget called himself a Muslim not because he obeyed the Koran, but because Islam was different from the white man's belief system.

When Midget finished eating, Myeesha decided to take him to the mall.

"Mrs. Helen, can you watch the children while I take Midget clothes shopping?"

"Sure," she said. "You two go ahead."

"Thank you Mrs. Helen," Myeesha said.

"I'll keep them for the night," she whispered. "Go enjoy yourselves."

The Ocean One Mall wasn't far from the Towers. So they walked. The casino executives put a lot of money into rebuilding and remodeling the Southside of the City where the casinos are located, but the Northside was left dotted with just a few new buildings.

"Where's the house that use to be right there?"

"The city tore that dump down," said Myeesha. "So much has changed."

The house didn't matter to Midget. He was thinking about the whore who used to live there.

They continued to walk past a man with bulging eyes and nappy hair.

"Midget!" the man shouted. "It's me Larry."

Myeesha shook her head in disgust over the filthy odor and kept walking.

Midget couldn't make out the face but he recognized the voice.

"I was in Rahway with you, two-wing, remember?"

Midget was shocked. It was unbelievable. Larry was a shell, half the size he was when Midget last saw him.

"Larry?!" Midget asked in state of shock.

"Yeah, man," replied Larry, cracking his voice with shame.

"What happened?!"

"It's the crack, It got me fucked up."

The Myth of Midget Molley   Ali Rob

Myeesha kept walking slowly ahead, not wanting to be near Larry's stench.

"Yo I-Kee, you gotta get yourself together," Midget said, using the Islamic term for brother.

"I tried man, this crack's crazy."

"No, I-Kee! You crazy for lettin' that shit do this to you, Look at yourself, I-Kee!"

"I know, but..."

Suddenly Larry took off running. He didn't get far. The police car backed up and slammed on breaks. A female officer jumped out and chased him down. Midget shook his head at the sight of the one-time track star being run down by a woman.

Midget quickly ran up behind Myeesha and grabbed a hand full of ass.

"I see a lot has changed," he said.

"Would you stop before somebody see you," she said. "Wait 'til we get home."

But Midget's blood was boiling for his wife.

"Didn't I say wait!"

"Damn that ass is big!" he growled

As they moved down New York Avenue, a limousine slowly cruised to a stop in front of Mari's hair salon. Midget looked on with curiosity as the children surrounded it.

"Who's that ridin' in a limo on the Northside?" he asked.

"That's Miss D." Myeesha answered.

"Who?!"

"Diamond DeWitt; everybody calls her Miss D."

"Who is she? What is she?" Midget shot off. "Is she a rapper or somethin'?"

"No."

"You know her?"

"Everybody knows her, She's the biggest drug dealer in the City."

"How you know?!" he asked knowing Myeesha was a square who never got out.

"Everybody at the job be talking about her."

"What do she look like?"

"She's pretty."

"Do she gotta fat ass?" he asked, grabbing Myeesha's booty with both hands.

"Midget, didn't I tell you to stop?!" she said, laughing as she punched him in the chest.

All the time he was in prison, Midget never heard about Miss D. Most of the stories on the Yard had to do with a strange new drug called crack.

Finally they made it to the shopping mall, located on the world-famous Boardwalk. It stood across from Caesar's Palace casino and next to Chicken-Bone Beach, the spot where Midget met Myeesha in 1972. Back then in Atlantic City, blacks and whites didn't swim on the same beaches. And it was by choice. Black people named their section Chicken-Bone because of all the chicken bones left behind each day. At night seagulls would fight over the bones until they were all gone.

The Myth of Midget Molley   Ali Rob

Midget took in the atmosphere of the mall. He was so into the scenery that he accidentally bumped into a tall, lean, model-looking man laying his mack game down on two young girls.

"Nigga!" exclaimed the yellow dude, "Watch where the fuck you going!"

Midget was about to apologize, but the man's soft green-eyes and high-pitched voice took him by surprise.

"Paul?!" Midget asked.

"Damn, baby! Hey, what it is?" asked Paul, nervously placing his thumbs in his pants.

"Pretty Pauline," said Midget smiling.

The two girls snickered, covering their mouths as they raced away.

Paul Benson entered Rahway State Prison in 1982 for assaulting one of his hoes in the casino. He received a five year sentence with a two year stipulation, but that didn't make a difference. In Rahway, each man was respected from the door. But Paul was only a pretty-boy pimp, not a gorilla pimp. One day a Five-Percenter named Wise accidentally wasted some coffee on Paul's well-creased khaki pants.

"Nigga!" Paul yelled out.

That was all the god needed to hear. In the boxing ring Wise was notoriously known as Left-hook Shorty. When Paul called Wise out, he let loose that patent punch knocking the pretty boy out cold. The booty-bandits leaped on him like wild hyenas. When Paul finally woke up, he knew something wasn't right. The cell-block was as quiet as a cathedral in the center of Rome. His pants were unbuttoned and he felt an uncomfortable wetness in his rear end.

At that moment, he had three choices: fight, fuck, or pull out. Paul didn't fight and he didn't pull out. He stayed in and became known in Rahway as Pretty Pauline.

"Whatchu doin' in A.C.? I thought you was goin' back to Pennsylvania."

"Come on Midget," he said. "You know a pimp go where the money is."

"I don't know about that, but I know a pimp will ho when his bitch can't," said Midget, laughing at Paul's nervousness.

"Damn, baby. Why you gotta hit me like that?"

"Cause that was some low shit you put on Brother Akbar."

"Come on Midget," said Paul. "I can't have the streets knowing what happened to me."

"But you coulda got him killed!" said Midget. "You know Big Wayne hated rats."

"He made out alright," said Paul, plucking his fingernails like a bitch.

"But it wasn't true!" Midget growled at this undercover punk.

"I'm sorry man," said Paul. "I'm just tryin' to stay on the low."

"Get the fuck outta here you little bitch!"

The Myth of Midget Molley   Ali Rob

Pretty Paul nervously strutted off, swinging his arms, pimp style.

Myeesha, who'd moved away from Midget and Paul, stood in front of Talk of the Walk looking at all the elegant dresses she couldn't afford in a lifetime. Playfully, Midget eased up behind her.

"That's real nice," he said, grinding against her booty.

"Stop it!" she said.

They locked arms and strolled along. Suddenly Midget felt Myeesha 's arm tighten.

"Wassup?!" he asked.

"Bitch!" Myeesha snapped.

The two women saw each other before Midget even knew what was happening.

"You better not say a word to that bitch," his wife snarled, snatching her husband's arm like a lioness.

"Who you talkin' 'bout?!"

"That bitch!"

Midget couldn't see who his wife was hissing about until Nancy bumped right into him.

"Hi, stranger," she said.

He was stunned. Myeesha snatched him so hard that the two of them nearly fell into one of the large flowerpots. Nancy giggled as she looked at Myeesha stumbling.

"You can't speak?" she asked him.

"Hold up, honey," he pleaded to his wife. "Let me..."

Before he could say another word, Myeesha threw

his arm down and angrily walked inside the Gucci Shop. People coming out of the Gucci Shop stopped and stared.

"Ain't that Midget Molley?" a lady asked the man she was walking with.

"Ohhh shit! That is him," he said.

"He's gotten so big."

"Eating all those potatoes and pumping iron a' do it every time."

"Well I hope he changed his life," she said as she walked her fat ass into McDonald's.

"Art told me you be home soon but I didn't know it'd be a week later," said Nancy. "Your wife need to calm down."

"Whatchu been up to girl?"

"Nufin."

They looked into each others eyes knowing that their past was about to resurface.

"Are you still stayin' with your mom?" he asked.

"Yeah; And you can call there and leave a message if you need some of this," she said, placing the shopping bag in front of her pussy.

Midget knew he had to go.

Nancy was a freak's freak, and that was exactly what he liked about her. She had some good ass and he was addicted. They'd known each other since they were children. She was his first girlfriend and his first fuck. Nancy wasn't the prettiest, but she had a work of art for a body and she knew all the ways to make a man never

The Myth of Midget Molley   Ali Rob

stop wanting it. Back in 1979, Myeesha caught the two at her apartment in bed. She tried to kill Nancy, but when Nancy didn't die, she tried killing herself. Midget ended up getting married as a way of saying I'm sorry, but nothing really changed.

"You better get in there with your crazy wife before she do somethin' stupid," ribbed Nancy. "Call me once you gave the psycho bitch some dick."

"I missed you."

"Yeah, whatever," she said, popping her chewing gum as she walked off.

Midget walked into the Gucci Shop only to see Myeesha being tongue-tickled by a tall, muscular man he didn't know. He was furious.

"Who "dis?!" he demanded her to answer.

Myeesha paid him no mind.

"Do you hear me talkin' to you?!" he barked.

"Excuse me, Bill," she said, turning to face Midget. "What did you say?"

"Come here!" he growled in her ear as he grabbed her by the shoulder.

"Do you gotta fuckin' problem?! Don't you ever let me see you gigglin' in another man's face! Do you hear me?!"

"You alright?" Bill asked.

"What if she's not, punk! What if she's not!"

Midget looked like a dwarf standing up to the six-three, two-hundred pound salesman.

"Pardon me, is everything..."

The manager stopped in mid-sentence.

"Midget," he shouted. "Midget Molley?!"

Other customers turned, looking in disbelief. A young dude who was clearly into the game punched his partner in the chest, causing his huge gold cha clatter.

"I told you that was him!"

"He look a little different," said the thin man with the gazal glasses.

"He was probably hittin' the weight pile, you know how they do."

People in the store pretended they wanted to buy something from the area where Midget stood. The whole city had been talking about him while he was in prison. Myeesha was like a hawk. She eyed two young girls who'd been pointing at her husband and whispering as he stood talking to the store manager.

"Damn girl, he look good," said Wanda.

"I don't care how good he look," Crystal said. "I want some of that money everybody said he got."

"All you do is sack-chase."

"They don't call me Miss Goldy for nothing."

"That gold-digging is going to be the death of you."

"I'll die one happy, wealthy bitch," she said as she twirled the diamond-ring around her ring-finger.

"Is she with him?"

"Who?"

"The lady in pink"

"I don't know but I'ma bump into him when we walk past," said Crystal.

The Myth of Midget Molley   Ali Rob

Myeesha sat on the edge of her chair, ready to get right in that ass.

"I'm Kevin," the store manager said excitedly.

"Wassup, Kevin?" Midget asked as he stared aggressively into Bill's eyes.

The young girl with the white see-through shorts and red tank-top bumped right into Midget. Myeesha jumped up like a kangaroo.

"Oops. Excuse me," Crystal said touching his well-shaped arms, "Is this your man?"

Myeesha's eyes were like two gun barrels staring through Crystal's silly teenage game. It was a look that only another female could interpret. No words were necessary.

The young girl smiled nervously and slid past.

"I'm Donaldson's brother from Bungalow Park," said Kev Midget, "Remember?"

"Yeah, tell your brother I asked about him."

"I wish you'd come on," Myeesha blurted out now annoyed by all the whispers and stares.

"My brother always speaks very highly of you," Kevin said.

"Don't you also got a brother named Tony?"

"Yeah!"

"Tell your people I asked about `em," said Midget

"I most certainly will."

Myeesha paid for Midget's sweat suits and sneakers that he liked and they left holding hands across the Boardwalk to the Taffy Store where she bought him a box of Salt-Watered Taffy, his favorite candy. Tourists from around the world came to Atlantic City for five things: the Casinos, the beaches, the Boardwalk, the Miss America Pageant and the Salt-Watered Taffy.

Next they went to Caesar's Palace. Midget was amazed at all the ass walking around on the casino floor. There was more here than on Chicken-Bone Beach. The cocktail waitresses wore togas similar to those worn in ancient Rome. But these outfits barely covered their asses. Midget's head spun left and right. Myeesha laughed as he walked around like a kid in Wonderland. The sounds of slot-machines ringing, red lights flashing and coins falling into the metal trays tickled his fancy. He smiled as gamblers yelled and hollered for the dice to land on their number. He pulled his wife's hand, leading them over to all the excitement. An old white man who appeared to be the center of attention at the craps-table was shaking the dice.

"Come on, baby; seven!" he shouted.

He rolled an eight. Midget rubbed his hands with animation.

The pitman gave those people who wanted to bet on the number eight the chance to place their bets. The signal was then given and the elderly white man was allowed to roll. The cubes bounced around on the felt-covered table and landed on number nine. All those who gambled their wager on nine were paid. Again people sat down their chips where they thought the bones would halt. The senior citizen lifted his pants and took

The Myth of Midget Molley   Ali Rob

a sip of his drink.

"Come on, eight, we need you!" he yelled as the dice flew from his wrinkled hand.

Midget and Myeesha stretched their necks to see if he hit it.

"Ahhh..." the crowd of gamblers and spectators exhaled.

"Here, baby, you throw them," the old man said to Myeesha.

She grabbed her husband's arm with both hands as the man held the dice in front of her. Midget licked his lips and nudged her with his waist.

"Come on, sweetie," the white man pleaded. "You look lucky."

Myeesha put out her hand and he gave her the dice. She nervously threw the dice without clearance from the pitman.

The big cubes landed on eight, a five and three. The crowd erupted with joy and applauded.

"NO ROLL! NO ROLL!" the pitman shouted. People were confused. Midget laughed and Myeesha became startled.

"It's okay sweetie," said the old man.

The pitman reminded them all that they can only get paid once the go signal was given. Myeesha had thrown the dice before she was allowed to.

"Come on, you can do it again!" the tipsy man shouted.

Everybody including Midget cheered for Myeesha as

she prepared to throw the dice. She picked them up and looked at the pitman. He gave the nod and she flipped them out of her soft, sexy hands. She watched with everyone else as the dice spun unusually long and then landed on double-fours. The crowd exploded with joy. Excited, Myeesha jumped in Midget's arms while the old white man slapped on her feather-soft booty.

"Give me a Kiss," he yelled out while pulling her close.

Myeesha just laughed, trying to pull away from him. Then the old man handed her ten one-hundred dollar chips and shook Midget's hand. They left the casino smiling and headed to their apartment on New Jersey Avenue.

Midget and Myeesha hopped on a jitney for the fourteen-block-ride to their humble abode. A few blocks from their stop, Midget's first cousin Annie boarded the jitney.

"Hi Midget, Hi Myeesha," she said

"Hey Annie," said Midget. "How you doin?"

"I'm alright" she said. "When you get home?"

"Today."

"You got so big."

"You think so?"

"Hell yeah! Look at you."

"How Aunt Dotsy doin?"

"She fine, How's Aunt Helen?"

"She's hangin' in there," said Midget, pulling the buzzer to get off the jitney.

"Myeesha, you take care of my cousin."

"I will."

"I know you gonna have a lot of fun with that," said Annie.

Myeesha smiled as they stepped off the small bus and made their way to their building.

"Home," said Midget as he climbed the stairs to their third floor apartment. Midget reached out squeezing Myeesha's butt. Aroused, she sat the bags down and nervously placed the key in the lock.

"Wait," she said giggling.

Midget's heart pounded against his chest as he pushed the door open.

His wife dropped her bags in the living room and ran straight to the bedroom with Midget following quickly behind her. They'd waited five long years for this moment. Silently, loving desire consumed them as they stared at one another.

As Myeesha stood up, they locked eyes. Their hearts beat wildly like drums.

Myeesha's succulent nipples perked up, seeming to say, "Kiss me."

Midget willingly obeyed. Reaching under her small shirt, he placed both his hands on her warm breast. Closing her eyes, Myeesha began moaning. Midget's dick crawled down his leg with anticipation. Myeesha began to shudder as Midget lifted her shirt and mouthed her left nipple. Continuing to tongue-tease her breasts, he slipped his hand down her shorts, fingering her until she couldn't take it.

Like a freak gone wild, she tore both their clothes off. Then she clasped both hands around his rock-hard penis and kissed all over his face, neck and chest all the way down to his pelvis.

Midget stood there like a king letting his queen do her thing. Myeesha's lips slid up and down her husband's chocolate dick like a hydraulic jack. He tried to slow her down so they could lie in the bed, but it was useless. Myeesha had his dick in her mouth like a baby with a pacifier. She wouldn't stop sucking. Everywhere he moved, she dragged along. He reached down and ran the palm of his hand over her hard nipple. She moaned and he freed his huge, hard dick from her mouth.

"Why you do that?" she asked with her lips glistening with saliva.

Her eyes were aflame with horniness. She stood to her feet and Midget guided her to the bed. Myeesha's untouched pussy blazed like a raging inferno. Midget rotated the head of his dick round and round the entrance of his wife's soft, wet pussy.

"Put it in baby," Myeesha pleaded. "Come on."

Finally he gave a hard thrust.

"Ahh," moaned Myeesha from biting her lip.

Midget fucked her with a wild rape-like frenzy.

"Don't stop," she kept begging.

And he didn't disappoint. Throwing her legs over his shoulders, Midget rhythmically slammed his dick into her pussy with penitentiary power. The sound of sweaty bodies slapping together danced around the apartment. Lifting her from the bed, he pushed her body up against the door and bounced to the wall, all the while pounding that pussy into a mushy mess. Surely the neighbors heard it all. But after five long years, the sex-starved couple didn't care.

"Fuck me!" she screamed. "It feel so good!"

"Yeah, honey!" he growled. "Is this what you missed?!"

"Yes, darling! Yes!"

He put his mouth on her titty and licked it savagely.

"Ahhh..." she moaned with pleasure.

Her head bobbed up and down each time Midget pumped her pussy.

"It's good ain't it?"

"Yes! Yes!" she cried out with a happy smile.

He put his hand in her mouth.

"I can't breathe," she mumbled. "I can't breathe."

"Yes you can!" he said carrying her over to the bed with his dick still all up in her shit.

"I'ma fuck you all night!" he grunted.

But his facial expression told her a different story. Pushing her knees to the side of her ears, he voyeuristically looked at his dick going in and out of her wet pussy.

Her breasts shook as Midget beat that pussy to death.

He pounded his wife one last time. Then it happened. Five years of backed up cum blasted into

Myeesha's womb like a rocket launching space. Finally released from years of sexual frustration, he fell like a lion on the Serengeti. But Myeesha wasn't done. Rolling over, she mounted him like a cowgirl on a stallion. Showing all her teeth, she rode that big, black dick all the way to climatic eruption.

Her body began to shake violently.

"I'm cuming, I'm cuming," she yelled out in ecstasy.

Pussy muscles took over, forcefully clenching Midget's dick and nearly popping out his eyes. Myeesha fell forward, keeping that dick right between her ass, refusing to let it go...

The next morning, Midget's brown eyes opened. He lifted his head and looked down at himself. Myeesha dogged that dick. He could see where she'd fucked him all night. He looked over at the clock. It was 9:07. He tried to raise his weak body up but fell right back down. His dick was still bone-hard.

"Myeesha," he called out.

No one answered but his echo.

Slowly he managed to sit up. But when he tried to stand, his legs didn't hold. As he dropped to the floor, the front door opened. The sound of women's shoes click-clacked across the floor. Fresh shopping bags rustled. It was Myeesha, but Midget was too weak to make his way to help her. So he just waited, sprawled out buck-naked on the floor.

"Why are you sitting there?" she asked.

The Myth of Midget Molley   Ali Rob

"My legs" he complained.
"Come on, let me help you up."
She grabbed her husband by his dick and he had a fit.
"What?" She smiled.
"I had enough honey," he pleaded.
"Give me your hand," she said affectionately. "Let me put you in bed."
"I'm exhausted."
"You'll be alright."

Myeesha helped him onto the bed then cut a sharp eye at his hard penis. As Midget's eyes slowly closed, she snuck from their bedroom to the living-room and undressed. When she walked back in, the only thing she wore were skin-tight red bikini panties and a red lace-trimmed bra.

Looking at him sleeping so peacefully, she smiled. Then she ran into the bathroom and got a warm, wet washcloth.

When her husband felt the warmth of the rag, he pleaded for her not to do it. But Myeesha blew his brains out and laughed loudly when it squirted. He lay helpless as she climbed on top of his dick. The pair proceeded to fuck the day away.

Before they knew it, it was late afternoon. Midget and Myeesha lay naked in bed as they talked about their future and how Atlantic City had changed so much.

"Promise me you'll get a job and not get caught up

in all that stuff again," she pleaded, lifting herself up to look down in his eyes.

He closed them knowing he couldn't promise her what she wanted.

"But you vowed to your mother," she reminded him. "Don't do this to us."

But Midget thought of the scores he had to settle and his addiction to the street life. What was he going to do, flip hamburgers for a living? A 9-to-5 wasn't his calling nor the way out of the hood. His philosophy was simple: *to you be your way, and to me be mine. Myeesha began to cry.*

"Things aren't the same," she pleaded, as if she really knew, "It's not the same honey. Guys are killing each other and robbing each other, it's..."

"Look!" he raged, "I'm not gonna live in this one-bedroom rundown apartment with you and our two children; we..."

"No sweetie," she offered. "The City's gonna give me a three-bedroom apartment and..."

"How long you been waitin' for that?!"

"Since Hyleem was three."

"How old is he now?"

"Yeah, but..."

"How old is he?"

"I know but..."

"Dammit!" Midget yelled. "How old is he?!"

"He'll be thirteen in December," she answered with a whimper.

The Myth of Midget Molley   Ali Rob

"Thirrteen?!"

"Yes."

"And you still got faith in those lyin' motha fuckin' politicians'!!

"I'm just saying…"

"Sayin' what?"

"That you don't have to get involved in all…"

"All what, Myeesha? All what?!"

"I'm…"

"No!" he shouted. "Have you ever seen me sell drugs?"

"But…"

"I asked you a question!"

"No!" she screamed, as tears streamed down her face. "I never saw you selling it, okay!"

She'd endured so much. She didn't want to lose another moment away from the man she loved so dearly.

"All I'm sayin', Myeesha, is that you and the kids deserve better."

"And so do you," she said. "You're bigger than that lifestyle."

"You don't need to be out there. The short-stories and letters you use to write me when you were in Ad Seg were so inspiring and uplifting."

He knew his wife was telling him the truth but the beast of street life was flying through his veins. While in Rahway, he'd eaten, slept and dreamed the streets. Like the Sirens of Greek mythology they called him.

Helpless to silence their voices, he constantly felt drawn to their rocky shoals.

"Don't throw away your life honey," his wife pleaded.

"Look, okay I won't throw my life away," Midget said.

Myeesha lit up with joy. She kissed him over and over again until his soul-pole rose to the length she loved, full erectile. Then she straddled it, bouncing to the beats of their hearts.

It was evening when Midget and Myeesha made it back to Mrs. Helen's apartment.

"Hi mommy, Hi daddy," said the exuberant Hyleemah. "Y'all been shopping for a whole day and night?"

"Look at your hair Mommy," said Hyleem. "What? Is it windy outside?"

"Yes, it's windy outside," she answered. "Now get me some water."

"How can it be that windy when it's summer time?" Hyleemah asked, smiling.

"Get your mother some water and stop asking so many questions," Mrs. Helen demanded. "And who was that who called here for your father?"

"Big Lou," Hyleem mumbled. "He said you can reach him at this number."

Myeesha stared at Midget as he recorded the number in his head.

She knew Big Lou far too well. He and Midget had been friends since 1975. They'd been dealing heroin

The Myth of Midget Molley   Ali Rob

since the 70's. Initially, Big Lou was Musa's drug supplier until he met Midget decked out in one of his trademark suits. When he first saw how Midget moved and controlled the drug scene on K-Y and the Curb, The 6'7", 300-lb Bronx, New Yorker laughed hysterically. He walked up and introduced himself to the Midget, thus beginning a lifelong friendship.

A few months before Midget caught his murder case in 1980, Big Lou was convicted of being a drug kingpin. His long money saved him from receiving a life-sentence, however he'd been snared by the Rockefeller Law, which gave him a five year release date but a lifetime on parole.

"He must have recently gotten out," Midget thought.

He handed Myeesha the phone number. Quickly ripping it to pieces, she flushed it down the toilet.

Chapter 3
SECOND TIME AROUND

Weeks passed. Midget kept running Big Lou's phone number through his head. But he didn't use it. Instead he found a job flipping burgers and dumping fries at Claridge Hotel & Casino. He hated that shit. The constant loud noises of the line-severs screaming for more burgers, more fries, more rice, more gravy, more this, and a little more of that drove him crazy.

"Fuck this shit," Midget thought to himself every day at quitting time.

Then each night he'd go home and vent his frustration by fucking his wife with raw, body-pounding aggression. She loved it. But for him it was no more than a quick fix, a mere substitution for his desire to hustle on the streets.

Every day he saw young teenagers driving by in the latest BMWs, Benz's and Broughams of every model and color. And every time, he became enraged. He knew he had the expertise and the credibility needed to rise to the top of the game, but the vow he'd made to his elderly mother kept him away from the life he loved. Still once a week, he'd always stop on the block to talk Mr. Kirkland.

"It's all about the timing," the old man said. "Take

The Myth of Midget Molley   Ali Rob

note. See who's who, learn who their suppliers are, find out how much product they're getting. This will prepare you for the takeover."

"But I can't handle this 9-to-5 shit!" Midget exclaimed, wanting to enter the game right then.

"Sit down," the old man ordered him. "P-five!"

"Proper Preparation Prevent Poor Performance."

"O-four?"

"Outwit, Outshine, Outgun and Outlast."

"W-three?"

"Wait, Watch and Win."

"E-two?"

"Emasculate your Enemy."

"R-one?"

"Rule."

"Power always rule Little Ceasar," said Mr. Kirkland. "You haven't forgot what I taught you, so why are you here?"

"Because I hate this job!"

"People often hate what they don't understand?"

"Oh, I understand bussin' my ass!" Midget complained.

"How do you spell believe?"

"B-E-L-I..."

He stopped spelling and the old man sensed he knew.

"That's what I'm trying to get in your thick head," said the old man. "You must put the 'I' before the 'E' to spell believe. If you put your emotions before your intelligence you'll never get to the top Little Caesar."

"I'm not happy," said Midget.

"Neither am I," the old man replied laughingly.

All Midget could do was return the laughter. Then the two talked for hours about the good old days of the 70's and how things had changed. Finally, it was time for Midget to go home.

Coming home to a one-bedroom apartment in the rundown Uptown neighborhood only incensed his bitterness. While in prison, he'd had his own cell to withdraw to when he didn't want to be bothered. But with two children and a wife, home offered no solitary space to retreat. However sex with Myeesha could always be counted on. The sexual routine was therapeutic for Midget until Myeesha uttered those three words, "I'm pregnant honey."

"What?!" he shouted, jumping off her naked body like the house was being raided.

"I'm pregnant."

"No!" he raged, as his dick glistened with her juices.

"Put it back in," she begged.

"What?!" he blared, dropping to the floor.

Another child was more than he could bear.

"I can't, honey," he mumbled.

Myeesha didn't say anything. She hated the thought of an abortion. She lost her very first baby and had never fully recovered.

Midget grabbed his head. His mind couldn't handle the thought of one more person in their overcrowded apartment. Tears of anger rolled down his face. Hurt by his reaction, Myeesha wrapped her arms around the pillow and cried.

"I can't," he continued to mutter. "I..."

Just as he was about to repeat himself again, the alarm clock flew past his head and smashed into the wall.

"You can't what motha fucka?!" She screamed reaching next for the lamp. "You shoulda thought about that when you were fuckin' me! You black no good son-of-a..."

Midget leapt to his feet, grabbing her arm before she could throw that lamp. He hadn't seen his wife this violent since the day she caught him with Nancy Barker. She looked possessed.

"Don't touch me you no good bastard!" she snapped. "You can fuck all those little teenagers and have babies all over the place but you tell me you can't. You can't what, mothafucka?!"

Midget was stunned. Of course there were always rumors of the nine children he'd fathered and he knew Myeesha knew of his two children by Vanetta and Jozetta. But did she know about the other four by the Spanish woman and that white girl from Somers Point.

"Who were you fuckin' the other night?! she shouted. "You think I'm stupid or something?!"

"No!" he quickly answered.

"Well why did you come home the other night and jump right in the shower before you even said a damn word?!"

"I'd just got off work!" he reasoned.

"Bastard, don't lie to me," she yelled, reaching for the lamp again.

"Hold up, honey!"

"I'll kill your black ass!" she yelled, swinging the lamp towards Midget's head.

"We..."

"We nothing! I took enough of your shit, I waited all that time while you were in prison and now you..."

"Hold up; listen to me," he pleaded.

"No!" she ordered. "You listen to me."

"But..."

"But shit! I'm having this baby!"

Two days later Midget was at the City Hall.

"Excuse me, sir," the young secretary said. "You can't walk in there without an appointment."

"Well Ms. Monica McClean," Midget said pausing to look down at the name-plate on the desk, "you tell the Mayor that Midget Molley would like to speak to him and I don't have a damn appointment."

Myeesha, embarrassed by her husband's outburst, tried to calm him down but he was tired of all the bullshit politics keeping them from getting a subsidized apartment. He also knew how Atlantic City worked. It was never what you knew but who you knew that got you places.

"Just calm down," his wife pleaded. "Let's wait

until..."

"Little Man," the mayor called out with a fake-ass political grin, "How's it going? Come in my office."

"Honey," Myeesha whispered as they followed Mayor Wilson into his office, "don't go off on him, please."

"Have a seat," the Mayor said. "Welcome home."

"Mr. Wilson, man," Midget uttered between hyperventilating breaths, "my girl been on the Housing Authority list for ten years and..."

"Stop right there," he demanded. "Myeesha, why didn't you call me or come see me?"

Mr. Wilson was the first black mayor in the history of the City. Prior to becoming the mayor, he'd once been Myeesha's elementary school principal. Every one knew and loved Mr. Wilson and was happy to have him as their mayor.

"I called," she said, "but they always put me on hold or said you were in a meeting."

"Twin," the mayor said to Myeesha as he leaned forward, "You could have come to my office."

"I once did, but..."

"Once?" he asked.

Myeesha bashfully pulled her lips into her mouth.

"Hold up!" Midget barked. "Honey, sit out there, let me talk to Mr. Wilson."

Midget knew the real man behind the titles. He'd given the man campaign contributions and paid him under the table.

"Listen man," Midget said. "I don't have shit, But I

donated a lot of money for you to be sitting there and I can't even get a fuckin' decent apartment! I'm stayin' in a one-bedroom shack with Twin and our two children and now she's pregnant again. We need a bigger place and..."

The mayor threw up his hand, motioning Midget to stop talking. He grabbed the phone and asked someone to locate Myeesha Molley's files.

"No!" Midget blurted. "Myeesha Hatchet."

"That's Myeesha Hatchet," the mayor said into the phone.

"Good, Good," Mayor Wilson continued. "You say she's been the list since '75? Gee, that's a long time. Get her a place ASAP."

A few days later Midget was still in his one-bedroom apartment. He was there alone thinking about how much everything had changed. He hated begging for anything. Bitter tears streamed down his face. Sounds of loud music from cars sped by and caught his ear. More and more, the vow to his mother and Myeesha was getting drowned out. Just as Midget found himself lost in thought, the phone rang. He didn't pick up, but looked at it, flashing back to when he was incarcerated. The guards used to rush in his cell-block, ordering the inmates to strip down for body-cavity searches. They'd poke their rib-spreaders into his side, demanding he bend over and open his ass cheeks. *What the fuck were they looking for anyway?*

Midget always considered it a tactic straight from

The Myth of Midget Molley   Ali Rob

the psychology of defeat. So humiliated, the men would jump at the mere sound of stomping boots and batons banging against shields. He wondered to himself how much longer could he deal with feeling like a prisoner on the street. The phone continued to ring as Myeesha opened the door.

She ran in and grabbed the wall-phone in the kitchen and began talking with Tyeesha.

"I just walked in the house," she said, assuming she was alone. "He must be at work."

Midget just sat in the next room not saying a word. Inmates are conditioned like that, to speak only when spoken to.

"How's he doing?" Tyeesha asked.

"He's alright, It's not easy adjusting but he'll be okay."

"Everybody and their mama wanna fuck him."

"Well you tell those little hot whores I said there will be no ding-a-ling for dinner tonight."

They both laughed. Midget smiled at his wife's praise.

"Do you know a girl name Judy?"

"Judy?" she echoed causing Midget's heart to drop.

"I heard these young girls in the salon talking about she had a baby by him and he don't know about it," Tyeesha said.

"That's his past, Tyeesha, and I'm not getting all upset about it."

"I know; I was just…"

"Plus I'm pregnant."
"Mommy gonna have a fit!"
"I'm grown!"
"But you know how she is."
"Don't tell her!"
"You gonna tell her?"
"Just don't tell her Tyeesha."
"How can y'all afford another baby or fit one in that small place,"
"Midget went off on the mayor."
"For real?!"
"Uh-huh."
"What Mr. Wilson do?"
"I don't know because he told me to leave."
"Who? Mr. Wilson?"
"No. Midget."
"That man is a fool," said Tyeesha. "Are you going over Mom's?"
"Yeah, I have to pick the kids up."
"Where are they?"
"Over Mrs. Helen's house."
"Midget coming with you?"
"You know how moody he is sometimes."
"Okay. I'll see you at mom's."
As soon as Myeesha placed the phone on the receiver, it rang again.
"Hello," she answered.
"Myeesha?"
"Who else would it be?" she joked.

52

The Myth of Midget Molley — Ali Rob

"Where Midget?" Tyree asked.
"At work."
"Tell him to call me."
"Okay."

Myeesha went into the bathroom which was off from the kitchen.

Minutes later Midget heard the shower come on. He walked in the bedroom, got undressed and strolled through the living-room and kitchen to the bathroom. Their apartment was that small.

She didn't hear the door ease open so Midget was able to watch the silhouette of his wife with perverted lust. His dick throbbed at the sight of her hand moving in circular motions around her nipples. He stroked himself as the pulsating water whipped her clitoris into a thick, stiff morsel of flesh.

She moaned as one, then two, then three fingers slipped inside her milky-way.

"Darling," Midget heard her whisper as his eyes molested the contours of her anatomy.

Myeesha tried to lick her nipple but her tongue wasn't long enough. Aroused by the sight, he grabbed his dick with both hands and started abusing it with psychotic intensity. Myeesha breathed heavily, turning the shower-sprinkler to full throttle and allowing the warm water to blast her clit. Midget stroked his manhood as he watched his wife's head fall back. They both exploded at the same time when suddenly, the door banged loudly.

"Police!" they yelled. "Open the fucking door!"

Startled, Myeesha almost fell to the floor as she rushed to get out of the shower.

Midget ran to the bedroom with cum shooting from his dick as he jumped inside his sweatpants. Just then, the door crashed in.

"Don't move!" the officer ordered Myeesha as she held the sheer nightgown around her wet body. With his hands in the air, Midget walked out of the bedroom.

Noticing how grotesquely long his dick hung in those thin sweats, Myeesha's eyes widened.

"Where the fuck did you come from," her expression seemed to say. *"And what the hell did you do now."*

"John, let me speak to you," the black officer said to the white one.

He pulled him out the hallway, glancing at Myeesha's erect nipples as he walked past.

"That's Midget Molley there."

"You're shitting me!"

"No, We hit the wrong apartment."

"That's Midget?!" the white officer asked.

"That's him."

"Fuck!"

"Take it easy," said the black officer. "He won't report it."

The officers apologized abundantly and left their names and badge numbers in case Midget and Myeesha wanted to file a complaint with Internal Affairs.

The Myth of Midget Molley   Ali Rob

The incident turned out to be good for something. A week later, Mayor Wilson came through. Myeesha was finally given a three-bedroom apartment in the Stanley Holmes, on Kentucky Avenue side. But for Midget, happiness was elusive. The immediate gratification of having a larger apartment with the woman he loved wasn't enough to fill the void. What he really wanted was the thrill of hustling and the fast women. To him, that was living. Again he took his frustration out on Myeesha, fucking her like a wild beast. And she loved every inch of it.

"Don't hurt the baby," she said laughing as his face contorted with each thrust.

"Take this dick! Take it!" he growled.

Myeesha giggled, knowing he was stressed about not being in the streets.

A few months passed and Midget's nightmare grew worse.

"Don't let it get to you," said Myeesha. "Go right downtown and see the mayor again."

"How she gonna tell you no man can stay here?! You ain't on welfare."

"I'm not thinking about the bitch myself."

"What else did she say?"

"I have to bring my pay-stub to the office."

"What kind of shit is this?"

"Those sluts just jealous!" said Myeesha. "All they want is for you to fuck 'em. Every bitch in this complex got a man living with them, but her fat ass wanna say you gotta leave or they'll raise the rent."

"How can they do that?!" asked Midget.

"Don't ask me!"

"How she know I was staying here?"

"I told you before I thought somebody was in here," said Myeesha. "The drawer where I keep my panties was ransacked. I thought you were in there."

"In there for what?!" Midget shouted.

Myeesha just looked at Midget like he was crazy, knowing she'd caught him sniffing her panties many times before.

"If I catch the bitch in here while no one is home, I'ma beat that ass."

"They got a key?"

"Yeah!" said Myeesha. "They have a key to every apartment."

"Well let's change the locks."

"We can' t."

"What?!"

"That's the policy."

"Policy!?" Midget shouted.

Policy was a word he hadn't encountered since he was in prison. It was policy to confiscate certain letters that Tyree wrote him. It was policy to wake him up at three in the morning to search his cell. It was policy to take his books, his clothes, his notes, his food Myeesha sent him, his mattress and even his life if he bucked against any of them.

"That's what they call 'em," Myeesha said. "Public

The Myth of Midget Molley   Ali Rob

Housing Policies."
"We gotta get outta here!
"Where we going?"
"I can't live like this!"
"What?"
"Like I'm in prison!"
"It's not that bad."
"You crazy!" he snapped. "How can you live in a place where damned peasants can come in and out whenever they want?!"
    Myeesha lowered her head. She knew sooner or later Midget would lose it. As he headed up the steps, she smiled. She knew his frustration meant she was about to get the fucking of her life. She ran to the refrigerator, downed a large glass of orange juice and double-stepped up the stairs.
    "We can move if you want," she lied. "I'll do whatever you want to do Honey."
    Myeesha wanted some dick, and she was going about it carefully. She laid her head on his chest and rubbed her hand down his stomach. Inch by Inch, his dick crawled down his leg. Her face showed her excitement. She went for it, slowly moving her soft hand down his cock.
    "*Got it,*" she said to herself as she mouthed his manhood.
    Midget took it from there, giving it to his wife doggy-style just the way the loved it, hard, real hard.

Four days passed. It was Friday, their day off from work. Myeesha stepped out to talk with the bitch in the front office.

After the negotiation, Midget was allowed to stay without the rent going up. The bitch had only wanted some attention from Mrs. Molley.

To celebrate that night, Midget's sister Trina picked up Tyeesha, Myeesha and him for a night of partying. He and Myeesha partied the night away. She loved seeing him enjoy himself without breaking the law. But what she didn't see was how the atmosphere of The Yacht Club triggered Midget's rush for the streets. So as the three women walked around talking about people, Midget found his cousin Jason and got to know the young hustlers.

"This is Link," said Jason. "You know Midget Molley, don't you?"

"I heard of him," said Lonny Rollins, known as Link.

Midget sized him up to be about sixteen, but it was evident he owned the club. The roman-arched mirrors covered the walls of the Yacht Club and were emblazed in gold with the initials LR. On each huge slab of mirror an image of his youthful face smiled. Behind the bar were bevel-stripped mirrors which sent beams of light across the dance floor and on to the stage where a wax statue of Link sat crossed-legged in a gold chair. In the hall area hung large pictures of him standing next to Miss America and a young looking Mike Tyson.

"This my cousin I was tellin' you about," said Jason.

The Myth of Midget Molley   Ali Rob

"Is that right?" Link said looking Midget over, nodding his head with the arrogance of a rich, young hustler as his thick gold chains and nugget rings sent beams of splendid reflections into the mirrors.

"Yeah," Jason said, "he the one that banged them dudes Back Maryland."

"Okay, now I remember," he said. "You know my brother, Punchy."

"That's your brother?!" Midget asked with exaggerated excitement.

"Yeah."

"Tell him I'm home."

"You the one they said killed Chuck and..."

"Yeah!" Jason shouted joyfully.

"I didn't kill nobody!" said Midget, looking around nervously. "That's niggas out here runnin their mouths."

"He cool," Jason said.

"Yo! Stop that shit I-Kee!" said Midget. "I ain't kill nobody!"

"It was nice meeting you," said Link, extending his hand.

"Same here," said Midget shaking the young hustler's hand with firm determination.

"Yo Jason," Link said. "I got that for you."

A pretty, copper-toned female walked up and kissed Link on the cheek. Midget screw-faced the female.

"*Where'd I see that broad?*" he asked himself.

"I'll be out in two days," said Jason.

"Alright, just beep me." Link said. "I got that for you."

He walked away with the young girl on his arm and a crew of young boys behind him.

Remembering when he had it like that, Midget nodded with approval. He wanted to get on bad, but he wasn't about to let the young hustlers get the upperhand.

Myeesha came over as Midget was snapping on his cousin for talking about the Back Maryland murders.

"Honey, there she go," Myeesha said stealthily pointing her finger. "That's Miss D."

"Who?!"

"The young girl Diamond."

"Diamond who?!"

His mind was still trying to figure out how he was going to cut into one of the young boys who appeared to be running things.

"That's Diamond DeWitt," said Myeesha.

"Okay," he responded nodding his head.

"She's cute."

"I see," said Midget, grabbing his wife's hand and moving closer for a better look at the heroin queen.

Miss D. was so small, about 4'10", 100 pounds.

He watched as she sipped from a crystal glass. Her lips were thin. Midget didn't know what he wanted more from little Diamond, her pussy or her paper. She was tempting in both ways. Seeing her reminded him of Vanessa Williams, the first black woman to win the

Miss America Pageant. Miss D. truly was a diamond.

Her shapely legs and the plumpness of her ass was a turn-on for any man. She wore her hair in a long ponytail which allowed Midget to see her face in full. She laughed broadly showing a set of pearly white teeth.

From her head to her toes, she was little but well-measured.

"See the girl right there?" Myeesha whispered.

"The one with the pants on?" he asked.

"No that's her sister, Mari; They're all part of Diamond's SGTO."

"What's that?"

"The Soul Girls Take Over."

"Is that what they call themselves?"

"Yeah, That's her clique."

"Which one was you askin' me did I see?"

"The one with the tight skirt on," said Myeesha, leaning into Midget as she pointed her finger.

"How could I miss her?" he thought to himself.

Her ass was like a full moon.

"Yo! Hold this for me," said Jason as he walked up to Midget, sliding him a five-shot .32-revolver. Midget pushed it down in his waist as his little cousin pulled a young girl towards the back of the club. Myeesha never took her eyes off Miss D.

"Yeah," Midget said, "I see her."

"They mess around," Myeesha said.

"Who?!"

"Her and Diamond."
"But I saw her kissin Wali."
"I know, but. . ."
"Are you serious?!"
"I told you things changed out here," she said. "You won't believe it but, everybody's licking on everybody."
"Ain't nobody lickin' on you, is it?"
"Not yet," she said.
Both of them laughed as they headed onto the dance floor.

In the club office, Link was getting the best dick-lick of his life. The young girl was in fact Crystal, the gold-digger from the mall.
She had all the potential in the world to be the next Naomi Campbell. Her long legs and thin frame went well with her sumptuous lips. She was delicious. All the young hustlers called her Crystal-the-cum-drinker. But they paid well. Her dream wasn't to strut, half-nude, down a Paris Runway but to suck her way to the top of the drug game.
Crystal gulped Link's gism down her throat and wiped the sweat from his forehead.
"Is it alright if I do that, Mookie?" said Crystal after taking her last swallow.
"Yeah," he said, kissing her passionately as he reached in his back pocket for his wallet.
Unlocking her lips from his, she walked over to his desk. Link fumbled the thin wallet for his driver's

license and Social Security Card.

"What's the number Mook-Mook?" Crystal asked playfully.

He handed her both identification cards and she wrote down the required information. Link got behind her and started grinding on her butt. She slipped the scribbled numbers in her purse and pulled her thong to the side. Whipping out his yellow penis, he pushed it between Crystal's pretty ass.

"Mmm..." she moaned, reaching under her legs to palm his balls. Aroused, Link pounded her with fiery passion.

"I love you," that stupid mothafucka confessed to the sack-chasing diva.

"I love you too Mookie," she said as Link let a load of cum shoot inside her overworked pussy.

Midget and Myeesha got home around 4 a.m.. They'd only been asleep for a few hours when a loud sound from someone laying on the horn blasted into their bedroom.

"Who the fuck is that?!" Midget said, obviously annoyed.

"That's those young boys blowing for those hot-ass little girls next door," said Myeesha, placing the pillow over her head.

Midget hopped ass-naked in his sweatpants and sneakers. He grabbed the gun from under the bed and raced out the front door.

"Yo !" he shouted, as he ran up to the burgundy 240 Volvo. "I got a pregnant wife tryin' to get some sleep."

"What!?" The young driver roared, leaning on the horn again.

"Yo, punk! You heard what the fuck I said," Midget snapped as he slid his hand around the pistol grip.

"Ohhh shit!" the passenger hollered. "Ain't you Midget Molley?!"

Easing his hand off the gun, Midget scanned the suspicious, young, dark-skinned face.

"Yeah," he said, "that's me."

"Yo, man," the young hustler excitedly uttered, "I'm Jerome! You know my mom, Gail and my Uncle Malik!"

"Jerome!" shouted Midget excitedly. "Come here!"

Midget grabbed little Jerome in his arms and smiled.

"That's Midget Molley?!" the young driver asked, walking over to shake his hand.

"Yeah, it's him!" said Jerome.

"Boy, I haven't seen you since you were a baby, Whatchu doin' with this?" he asked, pointing to the pager.

"It's for my girls," said Jerome smiling.

Midget threw him in a playful headlock.

"Your girls!?" he exclaimed.

"Yeah." he muffled.

"Yo, I'm sorry for blowin' the horn," the driver said.

"Oh," Jerome said. "This my peoples, Azeem, We call him AZ and they call me Ali."

Midget smiled. He could tell they were flat-foot hustlers.

"Y'all be cool," he said, plucking Jerome in the head. Then he turned to head back in the house.

"Yo, that dude had the flyest cars I ever seen," Jerome said.

"You see that old-ass sweatsuit he had on," AZ said laughing.

"He just got outta jail!"

"That nigga broke!"

"Man, he was a gangsta."

"I know, I heard my aunt say he's our cousin."

Jerome pushed his friend and fell out laughing.

"You aunt is a crack head."

"I'm not talkin 'bout Sherry, I'm talkin 'bout my Aunt Mary!"

"She smoke too!"

"Fuck you!"

"He ain't your cousin man."

"Wait 'til we see my aunt Mary," said AZ.

"We can go see her now," Jerome said holding up a vial of crack.

"Yo, fuck you man."

They both walked into the apartment next door laughing.

Midget walked back inside, sat down in the living room and had a flashback.

"LOCK DOWN! LOCK DOWN! everyone to their cells," blared the intercom. Midget knew what time it was as soon as the emergency alarm sounded. The

Special Operations Resistance Team, called the Goon Squad by the prisoners, rushed on to Two Wing in full battle gear-helmets, shields, bullet-proof vests, knee and shin guards, gas-masks, concussion grenades, pepper-spray and tear-gas.

Readying himself for the compressed grenades to explode, Midget opened his mouth as wide as he could. He was fine, but the blast busted the eardrums of those too dumb not to know that the grenades can only cause harm if the noise has no way out of your body. He stuck his head in the toilet and continued flushing it to lessen the effect of the tear-gas.

The guards were responding to a knife fight that had broken out on the tier of two-wing. A throng of prisoners tried to hold the Goon Squad back from the vicious battle between Brother Akbar and Wayne Patterson, the infamous butcher of Rahway.

Someone had slid a kite into Big Wayne's cell one day saying Brother Akbar was a rat. In Rahway a kite was slang for a note. Wayne, considered the rat exterminator of Two Wing, found the kite on his floor when he came in from work. Since that day, he'd preyed like a cat, waiting for the right moment to strike at his rat.

Brother Akbar was a loner, and from all appearances he fit the profile. No one mixed or mingled with him and no one ate or exercised with him. Whenever someone tried to be friendly with him, he'd screw-face them. He was his own man in Rahway. So when Big Wayne made his move, no one had his back. In an

The Myth of Midget Molley   Ali Rob

attempt to stab him in the neck Big Wayne missed, getting him in the shoulder. The sheer force of Big Wayne's attack caused Brother Akbar to stumble his cell. As he hit the back wall, he pulled out a 10-inch, finger-thick ice pick from his waist band. His right shoulder poured blood as Big Wayne giggled wildly from seeing the fear of death in Brother Akbar's eyes.

Teasingly, he pointed the knife at Brother Akbar waiving his left hand to try and snag the snitch by his sweater. As their eyes wrestled, Big Wayne swung the knife upward, missing Brother Akbar's chin. This was a tactic to spin Brother Akbar's hand downward in order to land his 12-inch shank between the loner's collarbone. But Brother Akbar had spent five years in Western and five years in Graterfords, two of the deadliest prisons in the country. Skillfully, he stepped in as the fake uppercut went past his neck, he hit Big Wayne under the arm, puncturing his aorta. The bully of the block everyone called the rat exterminator panicked and backed out of the cell onto the tier. Pint after pint of blood gushed from the huge hole. Finally the guards broke through the crowd. Grabbing Big Wayne, they violently slammed him to the concrete tier. Not realizing he was in mortal danger, two goons held each of Big Wayne's limp legs. One kept his black boot on his head and the other placed Wayne's enervated arms behind the back, cuffing him tight. With each heartbeat, massive amounts of blood continued to pump from his arm. Slowly, they carried him to the infirmary. Their deliberate pace ultimately facilitated his death.

Brother Akbar was lifted from his cell floor, handcuffed and roughly led down the tier by the masked ninjas. He stared at Pretty Pauline who stood in his cell dressed in a peach tank-top and a black thong with a snug fit around his ass and thighs. His lips were covered with red kool-aid and his hair was pulled back into a long, high ponytail allowing for his feminine smile and well-shaped eyebrows to shine in all their penitentiary glory.

Midget jumped as the ringing of the phone snatched him from his Rahway flashback.

"Hello," he answered.

"Salaama'laykum, I-Kee."

"Wa'laykum Salaam."

"Whatchu doin?" Tyree asked.

"Nothin," said Midget. "Just sittin' here daydreamin."

"About what?"

"Nothin."

"Yo, you gotta get your mind outta prison."

"Yeah, I know," he said despondently.

Tyree and Midget had been the best of friends since Jr. High. When you saw one, you saw the other. Tyree had once gotten hooked on heroin but, from jail, Midget helped him through letters of love and encouragement. Had he not been serving a 90-day sentence at the time, Tyree would have been with Midget when he killed Brian Collins.

The Myth of Midget Molley   Ali Rob

"Where Myeesha?" Tyree asked.
"Upstairs sleep."
"Somebody wanna holla at you."
"Who?"
"Hold on."
"Hello," intoned a familiar voice through the phone.
"Who 'dis?" Midget asked.
"Who it sounds like?"
"Kim!" he shouted out, forgetting his about wife upstairs.
"Yeah," she replied with a cracking voice.

Kim always did cry easily. The two hadn't spoken since the night she drove the getaway car from the Back Maryland murder scene. Midget had conflicting emotions over Kim. He placed the ride-or-die good times on the streets against the past five years that she'd never once visited him in prison.

But Kim loved Midget. During his sentencing, she snapped. She fanatically fought the deputies as they removed her from the courtroom. She called the judge and prosecutor racist dogs. Myeesha was there too, but she was too classy for that type of drama. She simply looked over at Kim, 17 at the time, and realized that Midget disappointed alot of people. She'd hoped five years behind the walls would change him.

"Where you at?" Midget asked Kim nonchalantly.
"K-Y and the Curb," Kim cried.
"Stay there!" he demanded, sounding worried. Midget double-timed up the stairs into the bathroom

for a shower.

Along the Adriatic Strip, gunshots cut the early morning air. Inside room 234 of the nearby Lincoln Motel, Gangsta Gee-Gee and Sassy-Faye had just finished licking each other. Startled by the blasts, the two ran to the window to see what was going on. All they saw was the Apartment Complex across the street. It was called Six Bedroom by its residents because each unit has six bedrooms. But hustlers from that project coined it Six Gun Territory because it was the most violent project in the city. It also housed more female pussy-eaters than Clinton's Women Prison.

The two women, who were both just nineteen, quickly got dressed and checked out. They footed it a block away to Red Klox bar to wait for Miss D. to send them a ride.

Inside the bar were other members of Diamond's SGTO clique who used the hole-in-the-wall to sling their heroin and talk shit. They had the Strip on Adriatic Avenue locked down.

When they first rolled up three years ago, all the male hustlers laughed and muscled their customers away. Miss D. contacted her supplier in New York and asked him to send Gangsta Gee-Gee and Sassy-Faye.

The two came to town and killed one person, David Barnes, considered the biggest heroin dealer in Atlantic City.

David supplied anyone who wanted some work, and he never told a person where they could push their product. Miss D. started that shit after having David killed.

Gangsta Gee-Gee was a shade away from being white and had strong manly features. Sassy-Faye was sable, sexy and seductive. Her soft gaze was a contrast to her concrete heart. Many unsuspecting men were lured in by those bedroom eyes only to be robbed, raped, or murdered. Her and Gangsta Gee-Gee had worked together in the mean streets of the South Bronx. Eventually they became lovers.

Gangsta Gee-Gee's and Sassy-Fay's murder of David Barnes was the talk of the town. They'd spent a whole weekend with him at his mansion in Galloway, a suburb of Atlantic City. He never saw it coming. The whole SGTO clique was on pussy. Every now and then they'd take a womb-sweeper to a motel for a real live dick down. The streets had it that David, who was about six feet tall, and weighed a measly hundred and fifty pounds, had a dick so long, the females who fucked him called it a womb-sweeper. As much as the Soul Girl's loved licking each other's pussy, there was something magical about David's wand that made them wonder was it really like that. Gangsta Gee-Gee and Sassy wanted to find out.

The pair fucked him with delight. Then they gave him an eyeful as they kissed and ate each others pussies in front of him. It was a great episode for him until they turned on him. Later that night, they butchered him with two hunting knives.

The Atlantic City Press called the David Barnes' murder the most brutal killing in the area's history. The gruesome act was disturbingly ritualistic.

The two SGTO members carried it out just the way their sick leader had asked them. They intoxicated David until he was unable to resist. Then according to Santeria, the religion of Miss D, they slaughtered David like a chicken. They bathed in his blood as it gushed from his throat. Then they severed his penis as a gift for the goddess, Diamond DeWitt. She kept this trophy in a thirteen inch jar of formaldehyde in her sanctum.

Finally Bertha, one of the young lovers of Miss D, arrived to pick up Gangsta Gee-Gee and Sassy-Faye from Red Klox Bar. She had no license but all the necessary skills to push the Porsche she was driving. They sped off heading to Diamond's home on the Westside of Atlantic City, the sight of many SGTO orgies.

On the other side of Red Klox Bar sat the Carver Hall Apartments where Marky V. lived and sold his crack. Seymour Jones had scouted the area for a month, learning all Marky's moves and weaknesses.

Each day he noticed Marky would take a crackhead in one of the buildings where drugs wasn't sold from. He stopped a girl named Carla and asked her why Marky did that. Carla told him that Marky gave them free crack if they gave him some head.

"TRICK," *Seymour thought to himself smiling.*

A few days later a silver two-door convertible Mercedes Benz parked on the South Carolina Avenue

The Myth of Midget Molley   Ali Rob

side of Carver Hall behind an old, black Chevy Impala. A young girl got out and headed towards the Tennessee Avenue end of the complex looking for Marky. Spotting him about to go inside building four with a broke-down broad, she hollered for him. Swinging her ass from left to right, she caught Marky's eye.

"I'll get with you later," he told the musky fiend.

He walked to meet the beautiful young girl he had been begging to fuck for years.

"Whatchu doing around here?" the good-boy-gone-bad asked.

"I need five."

"You smoke?!"

His whole face became alight with the possibility of having the girl of his dreams on her knees.

"Please don't tell Link."

"Tell Link!" he laughed.

"Yo, fuck that nigga."

She pulled out some wrinkled dollars and rushed him for her vials.

"Yo, walk with me over here," he said.

"Marky, I don't like being around here, plus..."

"Nah, you cool baby. I got something for you; Put your money away."

She walked with Marky into building four where he pulled out a handful of crack vials.

"I give you all of these if ..."

An old lady came out of her apartment and walked out of the building, leaving the door ajar. Marky held the young girl by the arm as he led her to the back of the small hallway. She slipped under the stairs and assumed the position. Marky smiled victoriously as Crystal Goodhead slid his little black pecker in her mouth.

"Wait til I tell bitch ass Link this," he said to himself as the gold-digging diva polished his penis with her warm saliva.

The door squealed as Crystal held his boy-size bone in her hand and looked over her shoulder.

"It's nobody," he whispered palming her head to guide her lips back where they belonged. Marky smiled with delight. Every hustler accept him, it seemed, had gotten head from Crystal. Now he had something big to brag about as her mouth filled with his excitement.

Suddenly the door flew open. It was Seymour. He looked around and started running up the stairs until he heard Crystal's voice echoing back down the stairwell. Following the voice to the back of the small hallway he caught Marky with his pants around his ankles.

"Bitch," he growled, beating the young hustler in the head with the gun as Crystal angrily spit his load on the floor.

Crystal emptied Marky's pockets of his work and pulled up his pants. Seymour gripped the kid's neck with one hand and kept his gun in the other. The three of them climbed the stairs to the second floor When they made it to Marky's unit, Crystal quietly unlocked the door and walked in. Seymour kicked Marky in the

The Myth of Midget Molley   Ali Rob

back with his size thirteen. The shitty-drawered youngster flew forward, crashing into the entertainment center.

"You know what it is nigga!" Seymour demanded. "Where the money?!"

"In the bedroom! In the bedroom!"

Seymour whipped him again with the .357 magnum.

"I'ma kill your bitch ass," he roared as he kicked Marky again in the ass. "Where in the room?!"

"I'll show you, I'll show you!"

Seymour cocked the hammer and turned Marky onto his back.

"Nigga!" he snarled through his teeth. "If the money ain't in there I'ma blow your fuckin' head off!"

"It's in there! It's in there!"

Seymour dragged him into the main bedroom. Marky got the money out of the closet floor and gave up where the drugs were. Crystal ran in the other room and found two kilos of uncooked coke hidden in a toy chest under a bunch of rubber ducklings and children's building blocks. Finally, they hogtied Marky and walked out of the building separately.

Marky lay still until he felt they were gone. Then like a walrus, he wallowed into the other room, knocked the phone off the hook with his head and dialed 9-1-1 with his tongue.

The emergency operator answered on the first ring.

"9-1-1, May I help you."

"Help!" Marky screamed. "I been robbed."

"Calm down," said the white woman.

"Please help me," he cried. "They tied my hands and..."

"Did they have weapons?"

"Ma'am, please send the police," he sobbed.

"I will but I need to know if..."

"Yes! Yes! Now would you..."

"Was it a gun."

"Just send the cops bitch. Yes!"

"How many of them had guns?"

"Help me, please..."

"I can't understand you," she said. "You have to stop crying."

"Jesus, please..."

"How many guns were there?"

"One!" he shouted. "One fuckin' gun!"

"How many people?"

"Two! Dammit!"

The door suddenly flew open. Marky screamed like a bitch.

"Marky Vincent," said detective Looney. "Take a look at this you guys."

All the officers poured into the bedroom where Marky was and exploded with laughter at the sight of the hogtied hustler.

Crystal Goodhead and Seymour Jones could've been the black version of Bonnie and Clyde had they not been so much alike.

"I'ma give you one kilo and $50,000," he said.

"No you not!" she snapped. "I don't know what to do with that stuff."

"Sell it," he said.

"I'm not selling that shit! Give me the money."

"I tell you what," he bargained "I'll give you all the money except fifty-thousand if..."

"The coke too?"

"Hell no, bitch!"

"Who you calling a bitch!"

"I'll keep the two keys and fifty grand, just give me some head."

"Come on, you ugly motha fucka."

Throwing the money on the bed Seymour smiled as he unzipped his pants. It didn't take long. As soon as Crystal put those cherry lips on his black dick, his legs started trembling. Just minutes later, he skeeted in her mouth.

"Mmph! You been eating garlic or something?" she asked.

"Yeah. Why?"

"I can taste that shit."

"Taste good, don't it?" he smiled.

"Fuck no!" she said, placing a stick of gum in her mouth.

When Midget arrived at K-Y and the Curb, it was packed. There were five fiends for every hustler. This was the life he loved, people everywhere doing everything. Music blared from Club Harlem, Wonder Garden and Sonny's Barber Shop. Children danced, played and ran up and down the street while the addicts did what they do to get a hit.

Boosters from near and far were on the block, selling and auctioning off their goods. The best shoplifter wn came through with her orders. She was no joke. Khalilah was her name. The streets had it that she could boost an air-conditioner in her girdle and walk from the store without any suspicion. *Bad motha fucka!*

Cars sped by tooting their horns at Midget standing on K-Y kicking it. Old friends and fiends laughed and joked with him like old times. And of course there were the haters who saw Midget as a foe.

"Yo!" Midget shouted to Tyree from across the street. "Where Kim?"

"She down by the School House," he hollered back while standing with Old Man Kirkland.

The Schoolhouse Apartments are on Illinois Avenue, one block from K-Y. They're called the School House Apartments because back in the early 70's the property used be a vocational training school. The school later lost its funding, and shut down. The city took it and the YMCA on Indiana Avenue and converted them into low-income apartments.

Once they were nice to live in, but you know how peasants are, they'll fuck up a dirt lot.

The Myth of Midget Molley   Ali Rob

Midget ran over and kissed his mentor on the forehead then walked towards the School House.

"What do he want with this girl?" the old, blind man asked Tyree.

"She been giving these little hoodlums sexual favorites for years."

"Who?! Kim?"

"Yeah, She's hooked on that crack stuff."

"Is that why she went to the School House?"

"Everyday."

"Oh shit!" he shouted. "Midget don't know nothin 'bout that!"

Tyree took off running after him.

Since school let out on Friday, Hyleem and Hyleemah had been over at Mrs. Helen's. It was Saturday and they wanted to go to Tyeesha's house to play with their cousins.

When the phone finally rang, Hyleem quickly grabbed it thinking it was his mom and dad.

"Hello !" he smiled.

"Let me speak to Mrs. Helen," said Big Lou.

"Hold on," said Hyleem. "It's my dad's friend Grandma."

"Bring it here."

Hyleem carried the phone to his grandmother, who was teaching Hyleemah how to play chess. She was such a precocious little girl and as grown as an oak tree.

"Hello."

"Hi, Mrs. Helen," said Big Lou with that fast, heavy-accented South Bronx voice. "Where Midget at? I gotta talk to him; I..."

"He's not here," she said softly, giving him a hint at phone etiquette.

"Do you know where I can reach him?" he asked calmly.

"You have a pen?"

Big Lou hollered for his mistress, Delora, to give him a pen.

"Okay," he said.

Mrs. Helen gave him Midget's home number. The two talked for a few minutes before they said their goodbyes.

Myeesha was pulled out of her sleep by the ringing of the phone.

"Hello."

Her voice was just above a whisper.

"Is Midget there?" Big Lou asked.

"No."

"Okay," he responded.

He quickly hung up without leaving a message.

As soon as Myeesha turned over to dose back off, the phone rang again.

"Yeah," she answered in a leave-me-alone tone.

"Mom, when you coming to get us?" Hyleem asked.

"Soon, Hyleem, Now please leave me a..."

"Where my dad?"

Myeesha looked around looking to see if Midget was still there.

"I don't know where he is."

"Do he gotta work today."

"I..." She scanned the room for his cook uniform. "Yeah, he's at work."

"You comin' to get us?"

"Yes Hyleem."

She dropped the receiver on the hook and slammed the pillow over her head, but it didn't help to block out the phone which rang again.

"Hello!"

"Damn ho, What's wrong with you? The baby kicking that hard?"

"Oh, Hey girl, What's up?"

"You still in bed?"

"I was," she said. "Somebody called here for Midget and ever since this damn phone been ringing."

"Where is he?" Diane asked.

"At work."

"Damn, girl, jail has really turned his life around; I wish it'd do something for that sorry-ass father of my children."

"My head is killing me," said Myeesha.

"When you due?"

"A few months."

"What is it?"

"A boy. God knows I can't handle another

Hyleemah."

They both laughed.

"Listen, I called 'cause I need to borrow your little black dress."

"For what?" she asked, rolling off the bed to her feet.

"None of your damn business," said Diana, jokingly.

"Bitch," Myeesha threatened, "don't get no cum stains on my dress."

"If I do, I know where the cleaners is."

"You a damn whore!"

"You just figured that out."

The two best friends laughed loudly.

"Who is it, Kareem?"

"Nope."

"Who?"

"Guess?"

"Bitch, who is it?!" Myeesha yelled, pulling her bloomers from her ass.

"I'za nota tells ya," Diane said mimicking a southern slave.

"And I'za nota gee ya de dress," Myeesha shot back. "How'za ya like dat."

"It's Anthony."

"Anthony D?!" she shouted inquisitively.

"Myeesha, girl that nigga can eat some pussy."

"That's disgusting!"

"You never had…"

"Hell no!"

"Midget never ate your…"

"Fuck no!" Myeesha said. "My husband would never do nothing like that. Yuck!"

"That husband of yours is a damn freak," Diane shouted. "Didn't you say he be creeping around sniffing your draws? Bitch, please!"

"What that got to do with eating it!"

"He put his face in it!"

"His nose, ho, his nose," said Myeesha.

"Nose, lips, it's all the same."

"Just make sure you take off my dress before you get to squeaking."

"Eeek!" Diane sounded with laughter.

"Bye, whore!"

"I love you Myeesha," she continued laughing. "I'm on my way over."

"Are you gonna use your car tonight?"

"For what?"

"When you go out."

"No," she bragged. "Anthony got a big 500 Benz."

"Whaaaat?"

"Yes, Lord, and I'ma be leaning low in that bad boy tonight."

"I need to use your car to go shopping."

"I'll leave it with you and catch a cab back home," said Diane.

"Okay."

Myeesha placed the phone on the hook and headed for the shower.

On the other side of town, Crystal finished signing all the insurance papers, completing the $1 million life insurance policy she'd taken out.

"It'll take effect in 45-days," said Mr. Washington, the proprietor of Washington & Washington Insurance Company, the largest black owned insurance company in the country.

"This is the best policy for those who wish to leave their loved ones economically secured."

"Do it cover all manners of death," Crystal asked.

"Sure," he said. "Even if you or him should slip on a curb and, God Forbid, die as a result of the fall, we'll still fulfill our obligations by paying the policy in full."

"And that will in..."

"Excuse me, you did name the beneficiary didn't you?" he asked while flipping through the policy.

"Yes, I..."

"Here it is, I see," he said. "If you should die, he'll receive your benefits and if he should die you'll be the beneficiary."

Crystal bubbled with joy on the inside.

"Okay. Thank you," she said calmly masking her excitement.

"No, I thank you, Ms. Goodhead. We're always here to help the people."

Meanwhile in the School House Apartments, Kim had just finished sucking Peanut's pecker and had begun glazing Junior's for some vials of crack when

The Myth of Midget Molley   Ali Rob

Midget stepped inside the hallway.
Why'd he have to see that?
He snatched the 15-year-old hustler away from Kim, causing him to hit the wall hard. Streaks of young cum released onto the floor of the smelly hallway. Peanut grabbed his gun and Midget charged him, just missing a ride to the other side of life. Another round went off as Kim hit Junior's wrist, causing the bullet to miss Midget's back. The small hallway came alive with grunts, growls and screams as Midget slammed his knee into Peanut's balls. The youngster yelled like a bitch. Tyree arrived in time to see Midget head-butt Peanut's face, breaking his nose. Kim continued to fight savagely until the third round blasted off from Tyree's blue-black magnum.

"Midget!" she screamed, as Peanut dropped his gun and ran up the stairs to his aunt's apartment behind Junior.

Kim grabbed the vials of crack off the floor, stuffing them in her panties. Then she raced out the door.

Later that day, Myeesha pulled Diane's car to a stop in front of her mother's house. Hyleem and Hyleemah ran up the steps and through the door. All the Hatchets from Farmville, Virginia were wn for the weekend. Ms. Rena held her daughter by the hand and walked her into the living-room for a private talk about the baby and the bills.

"Sweetie," her mother said, "how are you going to

take care of three kids?"

"Mom, is that what you brought me in here for?"

"You're on maternity leave for the next six months; how are the bills gonna get paid?"

"Midget got a job, plus I do get some money."

"That man don't make enough to pay all the bills Myeesha."

"We'll be alright."

"Where is he?"

"At work."

"Tyeesha said she heard people talking about seeing him hanging out on K-Y and the Curb; You can't..."

"Tyeesha need to mind her business and worry about that gay-ass man of hers!" Myeesha said. "Midget is trying and all people do is sit around and knock him; This is my..."

"No one is knocking him Sweetie. They're just concerned about you."

"No they're not, Mom! They just want me to...Ahh!"

"What's wrong, baby?!"

"My stomach! My stomach!"

"Lay down, it's just a cramp."

Myeesha followed her mother's advice and the pain subsided.

She rested until later that night. Feeling better, she decided to head back home.

It was about 10 p.m. when Myeesha made it back with the kids. Now she started worrying.

"Where's my husband," she asked herself.

The Myth of Midget Molley   Ali Rob

She put the children in their pajamas and let them go to sleep with her. She felt another knot in her stomach. She curled into a ball. Tears slowly rolled along the side of her face as she clutched her stomach. She didn't want to lose this baby. She reasoned to herself that Midget was working overtime, but her stomach pains told their own story. They'd been together a long time and she could feel something wasn't right.
"Call his job," she heard a voice say.
"But what if he s not there?" she asked herself.
So she didn't call. Instead she managed to cry herself to sleep... .

...It was about 3 a.m. and Kim was still alone sitting on the bathroom floor smoking crack. She ran water in both the sink and tub to drown out sounds of her inhaling the toxic blend of ether, ammonia and coke into her lungs. The shame and guilt of what she'd caused to happen sank under the weight of cocaine rocks she'd scavenged off the piss and cum stained floor of the School House apartment hallway. Her mind sailed away to a time when she and Midget were street-lovers.
She was an abused child who wanted to be out of the house, away from her uncle who'd been molesting her since age nine and her mother who allowed it to happen. There was no place to run. Before Midget, Kim was imprisoned in her own home by people who should've protected her.
By the time she was fifteen, Kim Mickens was

uncontrollable until she met Midget. When he was arrested, she was left back in the hands of the very monsters she'd run from.

...Myeesha rolled over and looked at the clock. She nearly went shock.

Frantically Myeesha reached for the phone and dialed her mother.

"Rrrrrring. Rrrrrring. Rrring..."

"Hello, Oh my god!" Ms. Rena shouted. "Where the kids?!...Stop crying, Stop crying! I can't hear you....Okay. Okay. I'll see you soon."

"Get dressed!" Myeesha ordered the kids through her teary eyes.

"Where we going, mommy," Hyleemah asked as her mother rushed her into the other bedroom.

"To your grandmother's house," she sobbed.

"What happened to daddy?"

"You heard what Mommy said," Hyleem grumbled. "Put your clothes on."

"Hurry up!" Myeesha demanded as she ran back into her bedroom, avoiding the mirror.

She heard a car door slam and quickly ran over to the window. It was Valerie and Eddie G, the couple across from her. Myeesha pulled away and caught her reflection in the window. Her heart was broken. She fumbled around the closet for a pair of boots. Midget's gun fell from a shoebox. Her finger slid around the trigger as she held it. She didn't want to live without him.

"Mommy," her daughter whispered, "what's that?"

"Go get your coat, sweetie," she said wiping her tears.

After placing the gun in her pocketbook, Myeesha grabbed her overnight bag and led the children downstairs. Hyleem listened to his mother while she buttoned Hyleemah's coat.

"It's nobody out there Mommy," he said.

Hyleem was a soldier at 13-years old.

"Okay, Come on ..."

"Let me go out first," he interjected.

Myeesha allowed him to be the man since his father was gone. She gave him the keys to the car and waited until he unlocked the doors. Then she grabbed Hyleemah by the hand and ran to the car.

Just as Myeesha turned the ignition, Seymour sped by. Their eyes bumped into each other. Seymour pumped his breaks. Hyleem looked over his shoulder as his mother pulled out of her parking space. Peanut and Junior were sitting low in the backseat of Seymour's Impala.

"Lock your door, Mommy," said Hyleem as he climbed over the seat to get in the back.

"Here." Myeesha said handing him the gun.

As she sped away, Hyleemah slid under her mother's arm.

The Bull Shippers Motel was located up the block from Resort's Casino on Pennsylvania Avenue. The two best friends had been there for hours talking about all the things that'd happened and how so much had changed in Atlantic City when a there was a deliberate knock at the door. Tyree pulled his blue-black magnum from his waist; the same magnum he blasted off in the School House Apartment hallway.

"It's them," he said as he peeped out of the window.

Midget nodded his head as he re-checked the two glocks.

"Open the door!" he snarled.

The three of them walked in and Tyree locked the door behind them. Midget held both .9 millimeters right where Seymour could see.

Peanut and Junior both trembled at the sight of Midget's eyes.

"Yo, Ahk," said Seymour, "they work for me, The incident that..."

"Check this out," Midget interrupted, "The next time these little punks pull out on me, I'ma..."

Just then, the bathroom door came open and Kim attempted to rush the two young boys. Seymour reached under his jacket and Tyree moved on him, placing his arm around Seymour's neck while pointing the barrel at his temple.

"I'll blow your fuckin' brains out bitch!"

Peanut and Junior sweated nervously in front of the two barrels that Midget aimed at them.

"I ain't got nothin! I ain't got..."

"Let him go, I-Kee," Midget said to Tyree. "He ain't strapped."

The Myth of Midget Molley   Ali Rob

"Sit down, punk," Tyree ordered Seymour.
The two kids hurriedly sat on the floor.
Kim, go back in the bathroom," said Midget.
"You gonna get yours Junior," she threatened.
"Just go in the bathroom!" Midget ordered.
She did, but not without throwing her shoe at the young boy's head.
"Listen, man," Midget said, "I called you here because Kim said these dudes work for you. I ain't got nothin' against you I-Kee, but if these kids ever do something like that again, I'ma punish 'em!"
Yo Ahk, Kim been suckin'..."
"I ain't tryin' hear that shit!"
"But..."
Tyree knew Midget secretly loved Kim. Even though Tyree told him everything Mr. Kirkland knew of his little freak from the street, Midget couldn't let her go and he wasn't going to let anyone talk about her.
"When you beeped me I thought you..."
Kim came back out of the bathroom with fresh smoke dancing inside the crack pipe in her hand.
"Tell him how you fucked me too bitch!" she screamed.
Seymour lowered his head.
"And tell him whatchu said you'll do if he said somethin' to you about me!" she frantically continued.
Midget walked over and pushed her in the bathroom.
"No, Midget!" she yelled hysterically. "He said he was

gonna kill you when you come home, Now say you didn't".

"Yo, Ahk."

Seymour felt trapped. Peanut and Junior put their heads down and tensed up.

They just knew Midget was about to start shooting.

"Go in the bathroom Mook," he said to Kim while fighting back the tears.

She tried to kiss him but he turned away.

"I'm not gonna smoke no more," said Kim as he closed her in the bathroom.

"I-Kee, it ain't no beef," Midget said to Seymour, "Kim need help and all I'm askin' you and your people to do is not to sell her anything."

"Yo! You got that," he said, jumping out the chair with joy.

Tyree grabbed him by the front of his shirt holding the gun to his gut.

"Let him go I-Kee."

Seymour and the two boys left. In the car, he counseled them on the art of deception.

"Fuck that nigga!" he snapped. "Y'all sell that shit to whoever you want! That nigga don't run shit out here."

"What if he find out we sold her something?"

"Just say you didn't sell her shit."

"But he crazy," said Peanut.

"Crazy people can die too."

"I ain't sellin her nothing," said Junior.

"Who you gonna get that can suck your dick like Kim?"

"A dick-lick ain't worth my life."

"Yo ! The next time he step to y'all about that bum bitch call me," declared Seymour. "If it wasn't for his brother, I woulda been got his ass."

"Who's his brother?"

"My man Yunus."

"Where he at?" asked Peanut.

"Trenton."

"Y'all cool like that?"

"Yeah! That's my nigga."

"When he gettin' out?"

"I think Yunus get out like..."

"That's his brother?!" Junior hollered, sitting up in the backseat.

"Yeah, he be home in a minute."

"They say he killed those people uptown."

"I was with him," said Seymour. "Dude thorough people."

"Their whole family crazy," Junior said "When my uncle found out what had happened in the hallway, he told my mom to send me down south to my grandma house."

"You ain't gotta go nowhere! You work for me."

...It was four-thirty in the morning when Midget walked into the empty apartment. He figured Myeesha and the kids spent the night at her mother's house. He undressed and dove into the bed. As his eyelids closed, the day's events ran through his mind. His ears rang with the voice of his mentor.

"The game is not like it use to be, Little Caesar," thought Midget recounting his mentor's advice. *"The streets have no more rules. These kids have shot their way into the game instead of earning their way. They don't respect those who went before them nor do they abide by the principles or the code of the streets. I envy the dead man."*

Old man Kirkland's words resonated through his whole body as he fell into a deep sleep.

Across town, Miss D and her SGTO Clique had been partying all night at her spacious home on the Westside of Atlantic City. The female exotic dancers she'd ordered to entertain her crew were just as perverted as her. There were more dildos than guns. They all walked around strapped up waiting to catch someone in the position.

"I want to see Sasha and Sassy make out," Miss D said with that cute smile of hers.

"Do you?" Sassy-Faye asked, looking at Miss D flirtatiously.

"I'd like to."

"Are you going to let us watch you and Bertha get down?"

"Ask her."

Bertha didn't say anything. She was the youngest of

the crew. Everyone knew Diamond was eating her pussy even though she denied it. There was so much pussy eating going on in Atlantic City that the men had trouble finding a woman who'd let them get some if they didn't submit to cunnilingus.

   The next morning Myeesha left the kids at her mother's house. She drove to the city via the expressway. She made it to Artic Avenue and cruised slowly, hoping to see her husband. There was no sign of him. Tears trailed the length of her face. She grabbed her stomach to comfort the unborn rebel who began kicking violently. The car pulled past K-Y and the Curb. She scanned left and right but all she saw were dead faces of crack heads and dope fiends. They all huddled around each other in the cold as the young hustlers handed out their medication in exchange for stolen loot.
   A red light stopped Myeesha from making a left turn at New York and Artic Avenues. She sat there biting her finger-nails.
   "Where's Midget," she cried to herself.
   Just as the light changed, a young, dark-skinned woman who looked to have seen a ghost banged on the car window. Myeesha jumped, causing the baby in her womb to stir.
   The woman's eyes were stretched wide-open. She looked paranoid. Myeesha pressed her brain for a name to match the face.
   She lowered the window just enough to hear the

woman's voice.

"I'm sorry, Mrs. Molley," she cried. "Midget wasn't..."

"You seen Midget?!" Myeesha shouted, letting the window all the way down .

"Yeah. We spent the night at BullShippers . "

Myeesha looked at her and knew she couldn't have been talking about her husband.

"Are you talking about..."

"Midget Molley," the woman interjected. "I'm Kim, remember?"

"Kim Mickens?!"

"Yeah," she answered shamefully.

"Where's Midget?"

"He's home."

"Okay," Myeesha said, wondering how the fuck she knew.

As Myeesha pushed the button to let the window up, Kim put her hand inside to stop it.

"You have any change?"

Myeesha turned to get some money out of her pocket book while Kim peered over her shoulder inside the car.

"Here."

She held up ten dollars. Kim snatched it and ran, nearly getting hit by a car as she raced to the School House Apartments.

Myeesha parked the car and headed inside the house. She felt her man's presence. *Most women know that feeling.* She slowly climbed the stairs as she pulled

The Myth of Midget Molley — Ali Rob

the gun out of her pocketbook. She walked in her bedroom. There he was, laying ass-naked. Myeesha stood there watching him sleep. Most of the time, he looked so handsome as he slept in their bed, but on this morning he looked guilty of infidelity. Her blood boiled. She picked up his boxers and smelled them. Then she smelled his dick. As she looked over at him, tears of betrayal freed themselves from her scorned eyes. Myeesha pulled out the gun, opened the revolver and closed it. Then she sat on the bed and aimed at her husband's head.

Clack! Clack! Clack!

Midget snatched Myeesha's wrist and pointed the gun away from his head.

"What's wrong with you?!" he shouted, looking at her as if he saw himself in the hell-fire. "You crazy?!"

Her eyes were blank.

For a whole week after that, Midget didn't trust sleeping around Myeesha. Even after he gave the gun back to his cousin Jason, he slept with one eye open. He didn't know whether it was the baby or his dick driving her crazy.

At the job Midget did his work well, but his antisocial behavior bothered the people who worked with him. They didn't understand why he only spoke when spoken to. He saw nothing wrong with his demeanor. He normally stayed to himself. But his co-workers didn't know his journey and judged him according to their experiences. In their eyes, he was crazy. No one told him this to his face. They sat around like slaves whispering about how he sat alone on breaks and ate alone in the employee's cafeteria.

"We can't have that type of personality around here," said Chef Sewell."

"I'm the best cook you have." Midget challenged. "Who can flip burgers better than me? Who can dump fries like I can! I'm the best!"

"Yes you are," he agreed. "But your co-workers feel uneasy working around you."

"Uneasy?!"

"They think you're..."

"Hold up!" Midget snapped. "I know Chef Cee-Cee ain't saying..."

"No. Chef Cee-Cee think you're great, but she no longer work on your shift."

"But I get along with..."

"That's not what they tell me Molley."

"I work well with others Chef Sewell. Please don't..."

"I'm sorry," he said. "We can't use..."

"Fuck you, man! I..."

"See," he pointed at Midget. "It's that attitude right there that we don't need in this fine establishment. You're fired!"

"Fuck you! I quit!"

It was pouring outsider when Midget left the job. The tumultuous rain drummed him with angry beats as he tried to cover his head with his little jacket. It was pitiful. Every time he covered his head, his back was

The Myth of Midget Molley　　　　　　　　Ali Rob

exposed. When he covered his back, his head was bombarded. It seemed like the whole world was working against him in some great conspiracy to make him snap. People drove past laughing. He felt they were laughing at him. Horns blared and he felt they were taunting him.

As he ran across the street, he fell in a puddle of water. A school bus filled with children erupted with laughter except for one little girl. Her eyes met his and embraced him. It was his daughter, Kenya. A tear fell from her eye as the bus pulled away.

Midget didn't what know to do. He'd tried so hard to please his mother and wife. He'd recently financed a new car for his mother and bought Myeesha a used one only weeks ago. For nine months he'd slaved over a hot fucking stove in Claridge Casino only to be fired because of some sorry-ass, handkerchief-head niggas who didn't like the way he stayed to himself. Now he was stressed trying to figure out how he'd pay the car notes and how he'd care for Hyteef, their new child.

"Pampers are high as hell," he thought to himself.

He was drenched, but that didn't stop the speeding car from splashing a pothole of dirty-ass water on him.

He walked into the house and his own children laughed at him.

"Look at Daddy, Mommy," said Hyleemah.

"What happened to you?" Myeesha asked as she walked into the living-room to take off his jacket.

Completely dejected, he pushed her hand away and

slowly climbed the stairs.

But things got better. April showers subsided and gave way to the May flowers. He quickly found another job. He now worked at the Show Boat Casino as a cook. But he didn't have to flip hamburgers and dump fries. His job entailed that he make the soups and sauces for all the buffet meals. Myeesha was so proud of him. He looked so good in his checkered pants and white Chef shirt, the standard uniform for all casino cooks.

Chapter 4
THE YACHT CLUB

Seymour was leaning against his Chevy Impala when Link's burgundy Brougham with ragtop pulled onto Gino's parking lot. He pressed on the loud horn and Seymour looked with curiosity.

A copper-toned arm waved from the passenger side. He smiled and limped over to the Caddy.

"Come here," Crystal yelled.

"Wait a damn minute," he complained limping as fast as he could.

"Link," she said, "this is my big brother I was telling you about."

"Stop playin!" said Link.

"For real. We like family," she said. "Tell him Seymour."

"She grew up around the way," he said. "Everybody uptown say they related to each other. What's up with you?"

"Ain't nothing, just coolin' with my girl."

"Yeah. She always talk about you."

"I know. That's my peoples."

"That's right!" Crystal smiled, tenderly squeezing his cheek.

"When you get this one?" Seymour asked as he stepped back to look at the brand new 1986 Cadillac."

"About a month ago."

"I gotta run; Beep me later, Crystal," he said. "Take care of my people Link."

"You know that."

Seymour walked into Gino's Chicken & Waffles to get up close on Miss D. He'd been watching her ever since he robbed Marky Vincent. Her empire was crumbling apart. Sassy-Faye and Gangsta Gee-Gee were arrested for firearms possession. They posted bail and flew to New York. Up to that point, they'd been the backbone of the SGTO clique. Diamond had a few other females to put in some work if it came to it, but none of them were as ruthless as Gloria Gunter and Faye Justiano.

Seymour's lazy eye twirled around in his head while the good one beamed in on the queen of heroin. She was looking every bit of royalty dressed in a pair of tight blue jeans, ostrich boots and a dark-blue sweater. The diamonds on her fingers and in her Rolex watch were dazzling, and she knew it.

"Give me a four-piece," she said to the young boy taking her order. "What you want, Bertha?"

"Two breasts and a biscuit."

Miss D. looked at her and smiled.

"I got two boobs and a booty," she whispered. "Would you like to eat that?"

Bertha pushed her gently as she looked around embarrassed.

Seymour tried to wink that lazy eye but it just

wouldn't cooperate. Bertha picked up the order and followed Miss D out the door. They hopped in the yellow Porsche and sped off. Seymour hastily hobbled to the Impala, speeding off in the same direction.

Meanwhile, Midget made a trip to visit his daughter by Vanetta, Kenya Anderson. She was the same age as Hyleem. It'd been a long time since he'd contacted her mother because she and Myeesha didn't get along.

Midget had lied to Vanetta to get her in bed and that's how they ended up with Kenya. But that was a long time ago. They were all so young back then, just teenagers. Still Vanetta basically wanted nothing to do with him.

He was from the Inlet section of the city and they were from a nice apartment complex downtown. She'd never met someone like him. Everything he didn't fight he fucked.

"What's up, Mott?" he playfully called Vanetta.

"Don't call me that," she smiled.

"Come here, baby," he said to Kenya.

She happily ran into her father's arm.

"I saw you fall in that dirty water," she said.

"I know."

"You looked like you didn't want to live."

"No, I was just..."

"Where you get that name Mott from Mommy?" Kenya interrupted.

"None of your business."

"Where she get it from Dad?"

"Her..."

Vanetta flew on top of Midget trying to cover his mouth as Kenya pulled at her arm. The three of them wrestled and laughed like they used to before he went to prison.

It was about 6 p.m. when Midget finished eating dinner with Vanetta and Kenya. She volunteered to drop him off around the corner from his house but he refused the offer, saying, "I don't want no one tellin' Myeesha they saw..."

"I'm not thinking about your sorry ass," she said as they stood at the door.

"You not?" he asked he as pulled her close and looked into her hypnotizing eyes. "Who you thinkin' 'bout then?"

"Not you," she lied, licking her lips in preparation for his.

"Mommy, can I go outside?"

"Go ahead," she said, never taking her eyes off her baby's daddy.

Kenya playfully pushed them aside and ran outside. Vanetta kissed him. Midget accepted her tongue and returned the favor. Her nipples hardened as his donkey-dick danced down his leg. Feeling it on her pelvis, her mahogany cheeks lifted to display a smile.

Midget nibbled on her bottom lip as he ran his thumbs across her thin eyebrows. She slid her hand

The Myth of Midget Molley — Ali Rob

down his cook uniform pants and pulled his soul-pole out and looked at it.

"Umm." she sounded while licking her lips.

He pressed on her shoulders, guiding her to the floor. Just as she was about to mouth his meat, Kenya busted through the door. "Mommy, I just saw Mrs. Myeesha on Ms. Diane's porch."

Midget spun around and Vanetta leaped to her feet. Struggling with his stiff dick, Midget stood in the living-room as Vanetta pushed their daughter back out the door, saying, "Okay, go ahead outside."

She bolted the door closed and giggled her way back in front of Midget with her skirt above her hips. His eyes blew up. He gulped and grabbed a handful of pussy. Someone rang the doorbell. She tried to answer it, but Midget wouldn't let her panties go.

"Bend over," he pleaded.

"Wait," she said. "Let me see who's at..."

"Move your fucking hand!"

"Stop," she laughed, loving every bit of his beastly aggression.

"I said move your fuckin' hand!"

"Stop, Midget."

He forced his finger in her tight pussy. Then She slapped him and he choked her in return. The bell rang again.

"Please, Midget..."

He was so excited by her struggle to get away that he busted off before running out the sliding glass doors at the back of the house.

Midget got home before Myeesha and washed his dick off. He was lying on the bed when he heard the door come open. Myeesha headed straight up the steps into the bedroom.
"Where you been?!" she demanded.
"Nowhere," he answered with guilt written all over his face.
"What time you get off work?"
"Like …"
Myeesha raised her eyebrows. Midget felt she knew something
"I just got..."
Before Midget could answer, the phone rang.
"Hello," Myeesha answered.
"Hyleem there?"
"Hyleem!" she yelled looking Midget dead in his eyes. "Hyleem!"
"Yes!"
"The phone."
"Who is it?"
"Who is this?" she asked, still staring at her husband with accusing eyes.
"It's me Mrs. Myeesha."
"It's your brother, Abdul."
"I got it Mom."
She placed the phone on the hook and closed the door. Midget's heartbeat picked up. He was about to

The Myth of Midget Molley   Ali Rob

spill his guts when he noticed the perkiness of his wife's nipples. She was obliviously wanting some. Silently he prayed his dick would rise to the occasion and his prayer was answered.

Two days later Myeesha was downstairs in the kitchen adding up the bills when the phone rang.

"Hello."

"Is Midget there?"

"Who is this?!"

"Trina," she sobbed.

"What's wrong?!" Myeesha asked.

"Midget!" she yelled after pausing to listen to Trina.

"I'm in the shower!"

Myeesha ran up the steps, pushed the bathroom door open and snatched the curtain back. There he was jacking off.

"What the fuck you doing?!"

"Nothin."

"Something's wrong with your sister."

"What?"

"I don't know."

"Okay," he said. "Go 'head out and let me dry off."

"Get your damn ass out that shower!"

"What do she want?"

"Take your black ass in there and find out!" Myeesha barked following him into their bedroom.

"Yooooo," he drawled.

"Mommy died," said Trina tearfully.

Midget's heart dropped and Myeesha could tell.

Those words, "Mommy died," echoed in his ear. They traveled through the chambers of his brain and repeated over and over again. But they just didn't register. He looked at his wife tal disbelief.

"Trina!" Myeesha shouted, "what happened?!"

"My mom," she sobbed.

"Oh God! Oh my God!"

Zombie like, Midget walked over to the closet lifted the gun from the hat box and loaded a round into the chamber.

"No, honey! No!" Myeesha yelled, dropping the phone.

As she fought him for the gun, a bullet exploded out of the barrel.

"Uh-uh," she grunted, twisting the weapon out of his hand. "Are you crazy?!"

He fell to the floor, drowning in a sea of emotions.

An hour later, Midget was being rolled out the emergency room at the Atlantic City Medical Center in a wheel-chair by his brother Art, followed by Myeesha and the children. The doctors sedated him with a large dose of valium and handed his wife a prescription for a milder antidepressant.

Two days later, the funeral came. Midget was so numb from the psychotropic medication that all the tear-dropping, arm-swinging, loud-screaming, floor-flopping, song-singing madness that normally infuriated him meant nothing. He sat there in a daze, staring at his mother's corpse. Childhood memories flashed

The Myth of Midget Molley　　　　　　　　Ali Rob

before his eyes. His thought of his first day off to school, seeing her smile as she pulled his little pants up and tucked his shirt-tail. He remembered her joy when he made the Little League baseball team, played football and participated in Boy Scouts. He could still sense her pride in seeing him become a paper-boy and an A-student. She'd had so much hope for him.

The guilt of never fulfilling her expectations pricked away at his conscience. Midget stood up and staidly walked towards her ivory-colored, gold-trimmed casket. Raising a psychotic smile, he eased his hand inside his suit-jacket. Myeesha's heart raced. She placed their young child into her sister Lynette's lap. The baby cried joining the sobbing and weeping of the multitude of Molleys' and others who'd come to bid farewell to their clan's matriarch and dear friend.

Midget looked over his shoulder one last time. His wife's face was covered with tears as she held her hands together as you do when praying, pleading telepathically with him not to do it. Midget pulled his hand away from the gun and slowly reached into his pocket and pulled out a piece of paper.

"I...I never knew death like this." he whispered. "The pain, the...the emptiness, the... the absence of her warmth, her...her wit, her wisdom, so many things that death robbed me of by...by taking her away at a time...at a time when I needed her most in my life. He robbed me of the only...the only wealth I had, I never knew death like this."

Midget took a deep breath and shook his head from side to side. Just as he began to read again, everyone gasped. It was Yunus, his youngest brother, flanked by a phalange of prison guards from the super-maximum penitentiary in Trenton. Stuffing the paper in his pocket, Midget ran towards his brother. The guards pressed in tighter, extending their hands, warning Midget not to approach aggressively. He stopped dead in his tracks. The hacks moved forward down the aisle with Yunus in the middle. Their number forced Midget into the pews. He fell into Mrs. Howard. Grabbing his hand, she strained to keep him under control.

"Your mother wouldn't approve of this," she whispered.

He pushed the gun back down in his waist and let the tears express his pain. Yunus raised his hands and mouthed a silent prayer as Muslims do when standing before the deceased. Then he kissed his mother and was led out of the church.

"Be strong," he shouted from the center of the mob that surrounded him.

"I love you Ahk!" Midget yelled back as Mrs. Waters pulled him back down onto the pews.

After the funeral and burial, Midget went home. He didn't want to be with anyone. Myeesha gave him his space but kept a protective eye on him.

A month passed and Midget continued to walk around in a depressed state of mind. He refused to take

The Myth of Midget Molley — Ali Rob

his antidepressants and was on the verge of losing his job. Myeesha's check wasn't enough to pay the bills, buy food, care for the kids and take care of him. Life became tense around the Molley household. They began to argue, fuss and fight. Then that dreaded phone call came.

"Hello," she answered.

"Mrs. Molley?"

"Yes it is."

"This is Chef Mansfields from ShowBoat Casino."

"Hi Chef Mansfields."

"Mrs. Molley, I explained to you some time ago that if your husband wasn't back at work soon we would be forced to..."

"But..."

"No, Mrs. Molley." he said. "We've held his position for..."

"He'll be day," she pleaded. "Please don't do this."

"I'm sorry, We already filled his position, He can pick up his three-day pay on Monday."

Myeesha placed the phone on the hook and cried. She didn't know how to break the news with her husband.

At that moment, Midget sat in Mr. Kirkland's living room playing chess.

"How many games have you already lost?" asked the old man.

"I beat him every game! Tell him, I-Kee," said Midget.

"Yeah, he got me," said Tyree.

"And if I wasn't the nice guy I am, I beat you the same way," said Midget to the blind man.

"Do you think you can handle the master?"

"Come on old-timer," he said, kissing the elder on the forehead.

"Set it up," said Mr. Kirkland."

"I'll punish you." Midget laughed while resetting the chessboard.

"You move first son,"

"I'll give you the honor, Pops, since you can't..."

Midget caught himself.

"The only thing I can't see is how big everyone said you've gotten," he laughed. "But when it comes to this game here I can see every move you even think about."

Tyree smiled as the old man took a mouthful of wine.

"Ahhh..." he exhaled. "Did he move yet, Tyree?"

"No. He's just sitting there figuring what color he want."

"Take the white," Mr. Kirkland said. "I like beating whitey."

"You ain't gonna beat me!"

"When he move, Let me know."

The old man sat back on the sofa and felt around for his lighter. He flicked it and lit a joint. With a sinister grin, the old man held his head back and blew the smoke up in the air.

"Queen knight pawn to Queen knight pawn 3," said Midget laughingly.

The Myth of Midget Molley　　　　　　　　Ali Rob

"King pawn to King pawn 4," he uttered, letting out a puff of smoke.

"Queen bishop to Queen knight 2."

"Queen to King bishop 3."

The old blind man laughed saying, "quit now and no one will ever know I beat you."

"Quit?" Midget mocked. "King knight pawn to King knight pawn 3."

"Some people gotta learn lessons the hard way." the old man said. "King bishop to Queen bishop 4."

"Queen Bishop Pawn to Queen bishop 3."

"He wouldn't listen, Tyree. Queen to King bishop 7. Checkmate."

"I won't say nothin about this if you won't," said Tyree,

"Next time I'ma gonna beat you in three moves," the blind man taunted.

"You good, but not that good," Midget conceded.

"Set the board up!"

"Nah, I have to go home and get ready for work."

"Go see Bo Diddle when you get a chance," he said. "Maybe he'll show you a few moves."

"Okay."

Midget rolled Mr. Kirkland back outside in front of Sapp's Luncheonette. Had he come out a second earlier, he'd have bumped right into the troubled trio, Peanut, Kim and Junior.

Tyree pulled his bomb on the side of Midget's spot and hopped out.

"I'll call you when I get off work."

"I'll probably be over Audrey's house," Tyree said.

"Okay."

Midget walked towards the door as Tyree drove off. A man with menacing eyes deliberately shouldered him. He spun around and snatched his gun out. It was Sonny, an original member of the BMC Boys. He smirked. Midget held the gun behind his leg. A thin, young honey-brown woman with dove eyes and Mediterranean lashes walked over and ended the standoff.

"Stop it Sonny," she said, locking her arm with his as she pulled him away. Midget looked down at the little seven-year-old boy the woman held with her other hand then cut his eyes back at her. It was Judy Smythe. He unlocked the door and walked in. There was a note on the refrigerator.

"Call me at Tyeesha's, Love, Myeesha."

He drank a glass of orange juice and went upstairs.

A block away on the Adriatic Avenue Strip, a smooth young hustler everyone called handsome AJ was slowly taking over the heroin scene. His method of getting money was a mixture of pimping and peddling. He didn't come on the block strong-arming, he came with the kiss and kick game, the way of Cool Breeze McMillian, a hood legend who had a stable of ebony and ivory ho's who turned more tricks than a ferris wheel. But like all people of power, Miss D. wasn't having it. AJ had already snatched Mia from her and was winning the hearts of Pasha, Portia, and Patra with his presence, his pimp-talk and his penis. Losing the block was one thing. Losing her bitches was another. She snapped.

Mia was on the Strip, sitting on the stoop of an abandoned building on Illinois Avenue with Candace and Candy waiting for AJ when a red and white ninja motorcycle sped by. The twins stood up. Candy walked a stone throw up the block to a phone booth. Her sister, Candace, ran across the street. Pam walked up.

"Come here, Pam!" Candy yelled.

"Hold up, I gotta ask Mia something."

"It's important! Miss D. wanna talk to you," she said, raising the phone receiver in the air.

"What the hell she want with me?!" Pam asked rhetorically.

"Probably the same thing she want with them," Mia laughed.

"I don't play that shit!"

"Pam!" Candace shouted at the top of her voice, waving her arm frantically for her to come across the street.

"Wait a damn minute!"

"Look what AJ bought me," Mia bragged, holding up her wrist to show off her diamond tennis bracelet.

"Damn, y'all gettin' it on like that?"

Before Mia could answer, a loud explosion sealed Pam's ears...

Midget hit redial. The phone rang three times before someone finally picked up.

"Hold on," the female voice said, dropping the phone on the table.

Midget could hear her talking to another person in the background. He laid there with his hand on his manhood.

"I'm back," she giggled. "You know I'ma cuss your ass out."

"For what?"

"Getting me all worked up for nothing. I'ma start calling you minuteman."

"Minuteman!?" he echoed.

"Yeah," Vanetta said. "Midget the minuteman."

"I thought that was Myeesha at the door."

"Myeesha at whose door?!"

"Your door!"

"That B..., I'm not even gonna go there."

"Please don't."

"You coming back over?"

"For what?"

"To finish what you started."

"You know I can't do that."

"Oh, you got your little skeet off messing up my skirt with that shit but now you can't do that, huh?"

"Come on, Mott."

"You know what!" she said, going up an octave. "You a sorry motha fucka."

"What you got on?" he replied, laughing.

"None of your damn business!"

She slammed the phone in his ear.

The Myth of Midget Molley   Ali Rob

He kept laughing until he heard sirens blaring outside. He jumped up and ran to the window. People were pointing and running towards the corner of Kentucky and Adriatic Avenue.

The Ninja motorcycle had violently broadsided a huge RV, instantly killing Gloria Gunter and Faye Justiano. The twins looked at each other in shock. Mia and Pam ran towards the accident and Candy screamed into the phone.

"What happened?!" Miss D. yelled.

"Gee Gee and Sassy!" she cried.

"What?!"

"They crashed!" she sobbed. "They hit a truck."

"Oh my god!" Miss D. shouted. "Come on Bertha."

They climbed out of the bed, got dressed and raced to the bloody scene. Seymour tailed them.

Mia stood among the crowd of people crying with the twins and Pam. They could see the black helmets and large dark faceguards that the two would-be assassins used to hide behind. Blood and fragments of their skulls filled the inside. An elderly couple prayed, calling on Jesus as people held on to each other in silence.

AJ walked up and pulled Mia away from Pam and the twins who were all hugging each other.

"Get over here!" he growled, "What the hell you crying for?! Those bitches was coming after you!"

"They my friends," she continued to cry as AJ led her to his car.

"Your friends?!" he shouted. "Miss D. begged them

to come down here to kill you and me! That bitch is sick!"

"Noooooooo…"

"Shut the fuck up! Get in the car! You so damn stupid you didn't see how those pussy-eating twins were involved. Had Gee Gee and Sassy not run through the stop sign, your stupid ass would be dead."

Midget turned from the window and its tragic scene and grabbed the phone to call Tyeesha.

"Hello."

"Tyeesha?" said Midget.

"Yeah."

"Where Myeesha?"

"Hey Bill, where Myeesha go?"

Midget could barely hear the voice.

"She ran to the store," said Tyeesha. "She'll be right back."

"Okay, tell her I called and I'll see her when I get off work."

"Her and the kids are staying over here tonight."

"Okay, I'll call when I get home."

An hour later Midget was at the employees' entrance where they punch their time cards looking for his. He turned to the time-keeper behind the cashier-like window.

"Have you seen my timesheet," he asked.

"Chef Mansfield pulled it," said Mrs. Nelson.

"For what?"

The heavyset, motherly figure just shrugged her

The Myth of Midget Molley   Ali Rob

shoulders. Midget got on the elevator leading to the production kitchen. He felt as if all eyes were on him. No one said a word. The doors to the elevator opened and everyone scattered off like roaches. He headed for the Chef's office. Chefs Mansfield and McKinley sat in the office smoking cigarettes and laughing when Midget knocked on the huge window facing the cooks' area of the kitchen.

Chef Mansfield looked at Chef McKinley. Their facial expressions were like, *what is he doing here.* Chef Mansfield waived him in and told him to have a seat. He knew right then something wasn't right.

"I guess your wife didn't tell you huh?"

"What?"

"That we placed someone else in your position."

"No, sir," he said, looking confused.

"Well we had to let you go because…"

"Sir, my mother had passed and…"

"But you know the casino must keep rolling," said Chef Mansfield.

"The people have to eat," Chef McKinley blurted.

"Sir, it was kind of painful for me when…"

"I lost my wife and son in a car accident," said Chef Mansfield.

"Well you should understand the trauma of it all."

"I do," he said, placing a bottle of antidepressants from his drawer on top of his desk. "And I understand that the world won't stop and wait for my wounds to heal."

"This is a business, Molley, and..."

"But I lost my mother!"

"So have I," said Chef McKinley. "This is a business and these casino executives can care less about your family and mine. It's about the money."

"Just give me one chance, please," he begged.

The two Chefs looked at each other.

"Step out for a second," said Chef Mansfield.

Midget smiled.

The other cooks were doing their job while Midget stood outside the Chefs' office like a school kid made to stand in the corner. He'd become like a black sheep. No one came near, waved, or gestured a sign of support. He may as well have been standing by himself.

Chef McKinley knocked on the window, motioning for Midget to come back in the office.

"Yes, sir," he smiled, believing he was about to be given another chance.

"The cook job is done," said Chef Mansfield.

Midget's whole facial expression changed.

"Don't..."

"Let him finish, Molley." Chef McKinley interrupted.

"The cook job is done," said Chef Mansfield "It's nothing we can do about that. But Mack tells me he has a pot-washing job he can..."

"A pot-washer!?" Midget shouted, jumping to his feet.

"Just until we get another cook position."

Tears of anger swelled in his eyes.

The Myth of Midget Molley   Ali Rob

"What are you gonna do Molley?"

His mouth moved but nothing came out. He knew if he went to the Union it would create a battle between them and the Chefs, which would most likely make him a management target.

"Alright," he mumbled.

"You'll take the pot-washing job?" Chef Mansfield asked.

"Yeah."

"Good!" Chef McKinley shouted, picking up the phone.

"I'll get you a cook job," Chef Mansfield reassured him.

"We need you to start right now," said Chef McKinley.

Midget walked out of the Chefs office and headed towards the pot-washing station. Everyone who knew or heard of him couldn't believe it, but it was true. Midget Molley was busting suds.

The pots were so huge and Midget was so small in stature that he looked like a kid. But this was no playing matter. After eight hours he walked home covered in grease, grime and grief. He avoided walking anywhere near K-Y and the Curb. He was so humiliated.

A week passed and Midget was still tip-toeing through the back streets to get home. Myeesha's job as a tour director wasn't paying enough to keep the family afloat, even with overtime.

Midget sat on the toilet toiling over all he'd been

through the past year since getting out. Then the phone rang...

"Honey," his wife yelled as he sat there in his own world. "Honey."

"What?!" he hollered, cracking the bathroom door.

"Somebody want you on the phone."

"I'm in the fuckin' bathroom!"

"It's Louie."

"Who?!"

"Big Lou."

Midget leaped off the toilet and ran into the bedroom.

"Hello!"

"Wassup?!"

"Louie?!" he shouted.

"Who you think it is?!" he laughed.

His Bronx accent sounded like a symphony to Midget's ears.

"Yo! Damn, man..." he said wanting to cry, "I'm fucked up Lou, I tried to call that number you..."

"That was the halfway house," he said. "They kicked me out and sent me to Attica."

"I thought you got outta Dannamore?"

"I did, but when I got sent back they sent me to Attica."

"Man these young dudes got the town on lock!"

"It's the same way up here but I..."

"Man, I been struggling and bussin' my ass for..."

"Just hold on," said Big Lou. "I'm workin' on some-

The Myth of Midget Molley   Ali Rob

thin' right now."

"Yo! I was so stressed, I was gonna rob this..."

"You ain't no stick up kid, You a hustler."

"I know but..."

"Just hold on," said Big Lou, laughing like he always did. "My people got that Boy but everybody smokin' that crack shit."

"It's the same way down here."

"I can get you all the diesel you need."

"That shit dyin' out down here," Midget replied. "I need some crack!"

"Don't do nothing, I'm waiting on one phone call."

"Yo, man, get back with me," he pleaded.

"I gotchu!"

"Louie, man..."

"What I say," he laughed.

"Man, these crackers got me busting suds and..."

"You gotta job?!" he shouted in disbelief.

"Yeah man, And I'm livin in the projects."

"Midget Molley in the projects!"

"Yo, I told you I'm fucked up."

"Yo! I gotta go! I gotta go! Somebody buzzin' the other line."

Before Midget could share the news of his mother's death with him, Louie clicked over to the other line.

Midget headed back into the bathroom. Myeesha placed the phone down.

After showering and getting dressed, Midget walked into the kitchen looking like he'd hit the lottery.

Myeesha stared at him with her sable eyes.

"What's wrong? I know you ain't pregnant again," he said, reaching into the cabinet for something to snack on. Then he looked in the refrigerator. It was empty too.

"Damn, it ain't nothing in here to eat. Whatchu gonna do about dinner?"

"How could you do this?" she tearfully asked.

"Not again, please," Midget complained upon seeing the load of tears falling from her eyes.

"No, not again," she cried. "I'm not going through this shit again, I'm moving on with my life."

"I heard that before"

"My sister was right, You ain't never gonna change."

"Well stop cryin' over me."

"I'm not crying over your sorry ass!"

"Blah-Blah-Blah," he joked.

"Get the fuck out!" Myeesha screamed. "Get the fuck outta my house!"

She pushed him so hard he fell into the refrigerator door handle, splitting his lip wide open.

"Look whatchu did," he mumbled as the blood dripped from his mouth.

"Get out! I don't need your good-for-nothing ass! Get the fuck out."

"Don't put your hands on me again," said Midget, using a paper-towel to stop the bleeding.

"Whatchu gonna do?!" she hissed, grabbing the broom.

The Myth of Midget Molley   Ali Rob

"Put your hand on me again and you'll see."

"Stay right there you black bastard!" she dared him as she ran up the steps.

With the quickness Midget ran out of the house.

He went to the the corner of Kentucky and Adriatic Avenues, laughing all the way. He spotted Kim and started talking to her about getting her life together when a black Benz pulled up and stopped.

He quickly moved behind the mailbox.

"Move Kim!" he said panicking when the reverse light came on.

"What's wrong?"

"Get the fuck out the way!" Midget said, pushing her.

The Benz stopped right in front of him. The dark-tinted window rolled down.

"Midget !" the young girl yelled excitedly.

"Bitch!" Kim called her as she crossed the street to sit with the other crack heads.

Midget bent down, looking into the Benz with suspicious eyes.

"It's me, Ellen, Rocky's little sister."

"Wassup Ellen?"

"You don't even remember me do you?"

"Nah," he smiled, showing his white teeth.

"Do you remember Rocky?"

"Yeah."

Saladeen and Baseel, Midget's nephews, pulled up on the other side of the street where Kim was.

"Well you should remember me," said Ellen, "because I was the girl you used pinch on the cheek."

"The one that use to sit on the porch?!"

"Yeah."

"Girl, look at you!" he said smiling "Get out the car so I can see you."

Kim fumed murderously seeing Midget hugging Ellen.

"Where's Rocky?"

"In jail."

"Whose car is this?"

Saladeen blew his horn; Midget looked in time to see Kim give him the finger. Baseel laughed.

"It's my brother's, He let me have it," said Ellen.

"That's a lot of car for a little body like that," he said, looking at her in those sky-blue shorts cut just below her coochie.

"I can handle it."

"I see that."

As Seymour's black Impala sped by, Kim flagged him down.

Midget saw his brake-lights come on.

"I gotta go Ellen," he told her and hollered for Kim.

She answered him with her middle-finger.

As they pulled off, Midget ran to his nephews and hopped in the backseat of Saladeen's bomb, a beat up car. As they rode the strip, two black and gold Ninja 1200's flew past, one right after the other.

"Damn! Who 'dat?!" Midget asked, turning to look

out the back window
"That's Nasheed and Khaleef."
"Nasheed?"
"Yeah, They from Bacharach," Saladeen said.
"Khaleef from Philly, I think," said Baseel.
"He be tellin' people that but I heard he's from Patterson or..."
"Damn. Who those young girls over there?" Midget interjected.
"They work for Diamond."
"I heard she on pussy."
"All those broads on the clit," Saladeen said. "She broke now."
"Who?"
"Miss D."
"That shit fading out," Midget said. "Everybody want that crack."
"Like this," said Baseel, holding up a small plastic bag.
"I know you ain't smokin' that shit!"
"Nah! We sell straight out the bag."
"I told you that when I saw you at the funeral," Saladeen said.
"Man, I was so zapped out I don't remember shit."
"That dude Seymour and AJ got most of the coke down here."
"I heard AJ jetted," said Baseel "That dude Anthony D. is moving a lotta weight too."
"How much y'all be gettin?" Midget asked.

"About an ounce."

"Y'all never had a kilo?"

"What's that?" Saladeen asked as he drove down Baltic Avenue.

"Thirty-six ounces."

"We ain't makin that kind of money," said Baseel. "But Sheed-Ali and 'em in V.A.C. be doing it like that."

"Do they be with little Jerome and..."

"You know Ali?" Baseel interjected.

"I knew him every since he was a baby!"

"Yeah. Him. AZ , AB , and Robby be holdin' down the Courts on Virginia Avenue."

"Our cousin, Akeem and his man, Lil. Bilal got the Brigatine Apartments locked down," said Saladeen.

"Where everybody gettin' their shit from?" Midget asked

"New York."

"Check this out, I just got off the phone with my man in New York and..."

"Word!?'

"Word is bond! He gonna hook me up and..."

"Yo ! Make sure you look out for the fam first," said Baseel."

"I'ma need you and Sal to move the shit 'cause y'all know I can't get out here."

"Oh, we gotchu! Just get the shit."

"Y'all got some people to help you move it?"

"Do we!" they answered in unison.

"If it's like that, it'll move itself," said Midget

The Myth of Midget Molley   Ali Rob

"Yo, stop by K-Y."

"That's the dope-fiends hang-out," Saladeen said.

"The money is on Adriatic Avenue and in the Courts," said Baseel.

"Virginia Avenue Courts?"

"V.A.C. all day and night," he said, holding up his rocks.

"I heard that broad be tryin' to run the strip?"

"That was a couple years ago. She ain't like that no more."

"Word is bond!" Baseel agreed as the car pulled into Gino's Chicken & Waffles.

Midget looked out the window in time to see Junior and Peanut pushing Mr. Kirkland in between moving cars.

"What the fuck they doin?!" Midget shouted.

Quickly, he jumped out the backseat and ran after the pair. Spotting Midget coming their way, Junior tugged at Peanut's shirt and the boys took off, leaving the old man in the middle of traffic.

Midget got there just in time to push the wheel chair from the path of an oncoming van.

"I'ma kill those motha fuckas!"

"No! Ceasar," the blind man shouted.

But it was two late. Midget chased the two kids towards the School House. Racing on foot down Artic Avenue, he turned the corner on Illinois Avenue going towards Atlantic Avenue and ran into Seymour and Kim. In one swift motion, he drew back his clenched fist

and followed through, dropping Seymour to the pavement.
 Kim tried to help but Midget kicked her in the ass.
 "Wassup, nigga?!"
 "Leave him alone Midget," Kim pleaded.
 "Bitch!" he yelled out, slapping her to the ground.
 Seymour pulled out his gun.
 Their eyes locked together in a deadly deja' vu stare.
 "I wish you would motha fucka! I wish you would!" Saladeen growled, pointing that big-ass .45 at Seymour.
 "Come on, Uncle Midget," said Baseel. "That nigga ain't crazy!"
 "Hold up Baz, Come here Kim." said Midget, pulling away from his nephew.
 "Nope."
 "I said come here!"
 "You don't..."
 Kim words sounded like blank noise as he charged at her. Seymour quickly moved out of the way.
 "Don't you ever talk back to me!" he snarled, kicking her as each word squeezed from his clenched teeth
 "I'm comin," she screamed. "I'm comin."
 Kim got to her feet and Midget pulled her to the car by her arm.
 "Be cool Unc," Saladeen cautioned him as he sped uptown.
 "Turn right here!" Midget shouted.
 "I'ma stop! I'ma stop!" Kim yelled.

The Myth of Midget Molley   Ali Rob

"Shut the fuck up" he snapped. "Pull in the alley!"
"Be cool,"
"Give me your gun, Baz!"
"Ahhh!" Kim screamed out wildly, breaking the side window with her feet.
"Yeah, bitch! I told you leave that shit alone, didn't I?"
He dragged her from the car to an abandoned building. She yelled hysterically.
"Yo, Sal, don't let Unc' kill her," Baseel pleaded.
"I ain't gettin in that shit," he said. "What if he find out she been suckin' our dicks too?"
In the building, Midget blasted Baseel's .38-revolver beside Kim's head. Dizzy from fear and the skull-cracking sound, she fainted. Saladeen jumped out of the car and ran into the abandoned building. When he arrived, Kim lay there motionless.
"Damn Unc, Whatchu do?"
"Get the fuck up!" Midget shouted, slapping her in the face.
Suddenly snatched from her unconsciousness, Kim complied.
"Now get your ass back in the car!" said Midget.
The two sat together in the backseat with Midget holding the gun to her side. Kim shook with fear as Saladeen drove down Pacific Avenue towards NARCO, the drug rehabilitation center.
"I don't get it," said Midget. "What the fuck's wrong with you."

"I'ma stop," she kept repeating through deluded tears. "I'ma stop!"

After dropping Kim off at the rehab, Midget had Saladeen and Baseel take him back home.

It was about 7 p.m. when Midget finally made it to his apartment.

"Myeesha," he yelled out as he walked through the door.

But there was no answer. Myeesha had packed his shit and left so he could grab it and leave. At the time, he didn't own very many items so she easily placed them all in the middle of the living-room floor with a long handwritten letter. Unfazed by his wife's efforts, he smirked. Without even reading the letter, he casually crumpled it and threw it in the trash. As if it was normal to come home to such a scene, he started carrying his clothes up the stairs only to be interrupted by the phone.

"Yooo," he drawled.

"Have your shit out of my house by the time I get there," said Myeesha.

"Okay." He hung the phone up and went back downstairs for another load. The phone rang again. He grabbed it.

"Stop actin' like a fuckin..."

"Yo!" Louie shouted.

"Who dis"

"Louie! I been callin' since..."

"Wassup?!"

The Myth of Midget Molley — Ali Rob

"I got it!"

"I'll be there!" Midget shouted with excitement.

"Call this number before you come..."

"Okay. I'll call you as soon as I line things up."

He finished putting what little bit of clothes he had back in the drawers and closet before showering.

After dressing, Midget strolled down the block towards K-Y and the Curb to talk to his old man. He walked like he was the king of the City. He didn't need anti-depressants to function, he needed the streets. He came alive whenever he was outside of the house. This is what he wanted. For him the streets were his happiness.

"It's on, old-timer!" Midget said, squeezing Mr. Kirkland's shoulder.

"I haven't felt this much excitement coming from you since the day you got out," said Mr. Kirkland..

"I contacted my old connect," said Midget

"The streets are yours, Little Ceasar. No one will be able to stop you but you."

"I can fight a gorilla, That's how good I feel."

"Push me over to the house," said the old man. "I got something for you."

Midget rolled him through the small walkway up to his door. The blind, old man gave him the key to let him in.

"Sit down," he ordered Midget as he electronically rolled the wheel-chair into the bedroom. Midget fumbled around with the chess pieces, placing the king and queen on the board facing each other.

"You don't want no more of that, do you?" the old man asked.

"How you know what be goin' on when..."

"I see with my ears son, You must do the same," he said. "This is for you."

"What's this?"

"Open it and see," he laughed. "That's what you got eyes for."

"Whoa!" said Midget rubbing his fingers across the stack of brand-new $100 dollar bills.

"You earned it."

"How much?" Midget asked.

"Who's counting?"

"Poor people."

"They have a reason to count," replied the old man. "What's your excuse?"

"None now."

"I wanted you to feel what it's like coming from the bottom again," said Mr. Kirkland. "That's why I didn't do anything for you in the beginning. You hadn't seen hardship since you stepped out here in '75. But for the past year, hardship's all you tasted. And you survived without killing yourself or anybody else. You earned this money. It's yours son."

Midget sat there with tears in his eyes.

"Dry your eyes, I have some people I want you to meet," the old man said. "Come out here Joe, Bring the rest of them with you,"

The Myth of Midget Molley   Ali Rob

Midget's whole face dropped with disbelief.

"You know these sorry motha...?"

"Take it easy Ceasar," the old man laughed. "They old friends of mines."

Midget looked in the faces of three old heads he could have killed on the spot; Chef Sewell, Chef Mansfield and Chef McKinley.

Midget had always felt there was some great conspiracy working against him throughout the past year. But never in a million years could he have connected all four ex-hustlers together.

Chef Sewell was tall, tan and sharp with the tongue. In the 60's they called him Cool Breeze McMillian. Midget had heard all about the hood legend, but he didn't know he was still alive. Everyone talked of him as if he was dead. But now he sat directly across from him smiling, in the flesh.

"Why they call you McMillian?" Midget asked.

"I'm the first mack to make a million off one ho."

"A million?" he shouted.

"You looking at the best of the best Caesar, crème de la crème," said Mr. Kirkland, sipping his wine. "These some baaaad motha fuckas here."

"What kind of pussy she had to get a million dollars?!" Midget asked.

"It's not the cheese that catch the mice..."

"Nor the the bait that snag the fish..."

"But the game of the bitch..."

"That make a mack like me filthy rich."

The four old gangstas erupted with laughter.

"What was your hustle Chef Mansfield?"

"Ask Killer Kirk," said Chef McKinley. "We worked for him."

"Who's Killer Kirk?!"

They pointed at the old, blind man.

"My old head?!" Midget asked screwing up his face with disbelief.

"Killer extraordinaire," Chef Sewell said. "He can shoot an apple off your head a block away."

"Blindfolded," chimed Chef Mansfield.

"If you want to be around a long time, you better listen to him," said Chef McKinley.

Midget sat there listening to the four old men telling him stories about how the game was played in the 50's and 60's compared to the 80's. They laughed at jokes that didn't seem to make much sense to Midget. They went on talking and smoking weed as if he wasn't there. He considered their younger days and wondered who they might have been had they not grew up in the gutter of Atlantic City. They all stood well over six feet. Cool Breeze was the shortest, standing six-foot-five. Picturing them in their youths as professional basketball players, Midget smiled. After kissing old man's forehead, he embraced the other three Original Gangstas and walked out with the back pack of money.

On his way home, Midget stopped in Gino's for some of their scrumptious chicken.

"Give me two breasts, two thighs, two biscuits

and..."

"Gimmie a four piece with that," said the female walking up behind him.

Midget spun around and looked her up and down. She was so close he could smell the perfume on her neck.

"Midget Molley, right?"

"Yeah."

It was all he could say. He was completely dazed by her beauty.

"You want me to pay for it or..."

"I got it," he quickly interrupted, digging in his pocket.

"Are you paying for the four piece too?" the cashier asked.

"Yes," said Miss D. "He's gonna pay for it."

Midget smiled at her. They walked out of Gino's together with Bertha jealously following behind.

"I'm having a party at my house," Diamond said. "I like to invite you"

"Is it alright if I bring my partner."

"Sure, there's only gonna be a few people there."

"Where do you live?"

"On the Westside," she said giving Midget the address.

"Okay," he said, looking down at the address.

"She'll be there too," said Miss D. as she got in the car.

There was something about Bertha that captivated

Midget. Miss D. noticed it too.

Midget walked into the house to find his clothes back in the living-room with the balled up letter placed on top of his things. He shook his head and prepared his ears for the sermon awaiting him upstairs. But there was no Myeesha. He searched the closet. She wasn't in there. He searched the other two rooms and behind the bathroom door. Still no Myeesha. He walked over to the mirror and read the message she'd scribbled across the glass.

"I'm tired of your shit! I put up with you for fourteen fucking years. Get your shit and get out! And I know about that crack-head bitch you been sleeping with. Get out! I hate you! Read the letter I wrote you no-good bastard."

Midget went downstairs and repeated his act.

First he balled up the letter and trashed it. Then he carried all his clothes back up the stairs and put them away. Then he picked up the phone and called Nancy.

"Hello."

"Is Nancy in?"

"No. Who's calling?"

"It's me Mrs. Barker, Midget."

"Oh. Hi, Hold on..."

After a long pause, someone rang the other line. Midget clicked over.

"Yo!"

"Get your shit and get out!"

He clicked back over. He heard Ms. Barker yelling

The Myth of Midget Molley   Ali Rob

for Nancy.

The other line buzzed again. He didn't answer it. The kids phone rang. He laughed and clicked over.

"Yoooo" he drawled.
"Salaama'laykum."
"Who dis?!, Yunus?!"
"Yeah."
"Where you at?!"
"I'm home."
"Trina told me you wasn't getin'out 'til…"
"I'm on furlough."
"From Trenton?!" Midget shouted.
"Nah," he laughed. "I been in Leesburg for two months."
"When you gotta go back?"
"Sunday."
"You gotta whole weekend pass?"
"Yeah."
"Where Tina?"
"She right here."
"Your daughters too."
"Yeah."
"You talked to the family?"
"Yeah, I caught most of them over Trina's house," he said. "Why you haven't been uch with them?"
"I don't know. Damn!"
"What?"
"I have somebody on the other line; Hold on!"
"I need to holla at you about Seymour," said Yunus.

"Okay."
Midget clicked over to the other line.
"Hello!" he yelled.
"The next time I'ma hang up!" Nancy said. "I was getting my hair braided."
"Wassup, baby?"
"You must want some ass?"
Yunus clicked to his other line and called Seymour.
"Yo!" Seymour answered.
"I-Kee."
"Yeah."
"I didn't get a chance to talk to him about it, but finish tellin' me about that thing," said Yunus.
"Yo Ahk, you gotta talk to him man," said Seymour. "He stole me."
"I told you, I got that."
"He trippin' about that bum bitch, Kim."
"Kim Mickens?"
"Yeah!" he said. "She around givin' the whole city some head and he threatening my little mans and 'em."
"Why you ain't do that?"
"I was but the way he's trippin' he gonna come right at me."
"You know where she be at?"
"She in the program."
"NARCO?"
"Yeah."
"That's good," Yunus said. "At least she's tryin' clean herself up."

The Myth of Midget Molley — Ali Rob

"Man, that ho be creepin' outta there every night."

"She still gettin' high?"

"I had her and another female from the program over here a couple days ago."

"Yo Ahk, I'ma tell you what she told me," Seymour said. "Midget threatened to kill her that's the only reason why she's stayin' in the program, just so he won't go off. But she's always creepin' around at night."

"I'll take care of that for you," Yunus said. "Now finish tellin me about that thing you got set up."

"It's easy!"

"How many people?"

"About six; No more than ten," said Seymour. "All females."

"How much?"

"The bitch was just gettin' off the ground when you got sent back. But now the bitch got it like that."

"Like how much?"

"At least a key of Boy and about two hundred thou."

"Oh yeah?"

"Word is bond!"

"You did all the..."

"Everything! I did everything," he boasted. "You remember Vernon?"

"Fat Vernon Lyons?" Yunus laughed.

"Yeah, he own this nice club over there on New York Avenue."

"New York Avenue? Where on New York Avenue?!"

"By the Boardwalk."

"I thought that was the Chez Paree?"

"They remodeled it and changed the name to the Blue Light."

"Okay."

"Yo! Vernon let me up in the VIP to watch her every move."

"I ain't got noth work with and..."

"I got all the firepower we need," he interjected

"What kind of security she got?"

"She gotta little bullshit camera system but it..."

"No guns?"

"Yeah. She gotta little crew that'll put some work in but you know how we get down."

"We gotta do it before I go back. This way 'case some thin' go wrong, I gotta good alibi."

"When you gotta be back?"

"Sunday."

"I wanted to hit her tonight," said Seymour. "She havin' a little after-party at her house."

"How you know?"

They continued talking about the caper Seymour wanted so desperately to pull off. On the other line, Nancy and Midget talked away about hooking up at the Yacht Club.

"I'll be there," she said. "Just make sure you be there!"

"What time you comin?" he asked.

"My name is not Myeesha! So don't be puttin' me on no damn clock!

The Myth of Midget Molley — Ali Rob

"I'ma be there about one."

"That's on you."

"Why you playin' fuckin' games!"

"Who you cussin at!"

"I asked..." CLICK. She slammed the phone right in his ear.

Midget trusted no one carrying his drugs from New York the way he trusted Nancy. She'd packed many a bundle of heroin in her girdle back in the 70's. Now he was trying to work what little magic he had left on his first girlfriend.

He sat the phone on the night table and started counting the last of what the old man gave him. Hearing someone come in the front door, he quickly put the money back in the back pack as Myeesha raced up the stairs.

"Didn't I tell you to get your shit outta my house,"

"Yeah."

"Well get it the fuck out!" Myeesha shouted.

He looked at her like she was crazy.

"Did you hear what I said?"

"Yep," he said, laying back on the bed with his hands behind his head smiling at her.

"Oh, you think it's a joke huh?!"

She started pulling his clothes from the drawers, throwing them on the floor and out into the hallway.

"You gettin' the fuck outta here!" she thundered.

He got up and walked into the bathroom. She threatened him again. "And I'm filing for a fuckin' divorce too!"

He couldn't hear her due to the sounds from the shower and he couldn't see the angry tears rolling down her face.

"I'm tired of his shit," she mumbled to herself. *"I waited all this fuckin' time and he get out here and do..."*

"Wear you throw my boxers?" he asked.

Myeesha turned around trying her best to focus on his face, but her eyes betrayed her, bouncing from his balls to his brown bedroom eyes. He was naked and dripping with water. Her heart pounded. Beads of water fell from his face and chiseled body.

"They under there," she said, pointing to the pile of stuff on the floor.

He stared at her as she slowly searched his underclothes until she found a pair of his boxers. For Myeesha anger no longer mattered. All she wanted now was to be loved. With passion, Midget sexed her until they both fell asleep.

After a few hours the phone rang like an alarm clock. Myeesha stretched her arm.

"Hello," she answered groggily.

"Hey Myeesha, where Midget?"

"Hold on," she said as she turned to give him the phone.

"Yo," he grunted into the phone.

"Whatchu doin?!"

"Why you talkin' so loud?"

"Get up, man! It's ten after one," said Tyree. "I been

The Myth of Midget Molley Ali Rob

knocking on the door for like..."
"Where you at?"
"At the phone-booth on Illinois and Adriatic."
"Come on over, I'm up."
"Don't fall back to sleep."
"I'll unlock the door,"
"No! I saw Sonny's punk ass walking past there when I first pulled up."
"Walking past where?!" Midget asked, jumping out of the bed.
"I'll be right there," Tyree said.
Midget looked down at Myeesha as she slept. She'd endured so much of his bullshit. He knew she was the best woman for him and the only one woman who truly loved him for who he was internally. But he was addicted to the street life. He just couldn't shake it.

Midget and Tyree arrived at the Yacht Club an hour later. It was in full swing. Eric B. and Rakim blasted through the huge speaker system and the young women were throwing their asses like beach balls. Tyree nudged Midget with his elbow to look ahead in the crowd. It was Seymour, sitting incognito with Crystal.
"That broad look familiar," said Midget
"Which one?" Tyree asked.
"The one with Seymour."
"That's Crystal!"
"You know her?"

"That's the bitch that set up Marky Vincent, I told you about her a while ago."

"I seen her somewhere."

Link walked over to Crystal and Seymour.

"Yeah," Midget said, shaking his head. "That's where I remember her from, the mall. She was in the Gucci Shop when I first got out. Then I saw her in here the last time I came through."

"The bitch is a freak."

"Watch my back."

"Where you goin?!"

I'ma holla at..."

"There's Nancy," said Tyree.

"Where?!"

Midget looked over his shoulder. She'd just sashayed through the doorway. Link headed for his office.

From the VIP, Crystal and Seymour continued scheming.

"Can you get Miss D. to change the party to Sunday?" Seymour asked.

"I can't get the bitch to do shit. Link said he's taking me there tonight. So if you don't want to do it, I'll get Freddie B. and Kalvin G. to do it."

"No. I got my man coming with me."

"Who?"

"Yunus."

"Yunus!" she echoed.

"Yeah, Midget Molley's brother."
"I heard Diamond tell Link Midget was coming too."
"Word?!"
Seymour sat straight up on the sofa.
"That's what she said."
"I'ma get his ass."
"For what?" Crystal asked.
"That nigga shot me," he said, lifting up his pant leg to show the bullet wound.
"When he do that?"
"Before he went to jail," he replied. "If it wasn't for his brother, I woulda got his ass back then."
"I wanna rob his ass, I heard he got a lot of money."
"That nigga broke!"
"Yo Seymour!" Cory yelled. "Over here!"
He waved for him to come to the security booth.
Seymour threw his hands up like, *what s up?*
"Somebody want you at the door!"
Midget cut his eyes at Cory as Seymour walked towards him and out the door. Crystal sat on the love-sofa by herself with her little hands covering what her little skirt didn't. Opportunity struck as Midget walked over and introduced himself.
"Don't I know you from somewhere?"
"I'm Link's girlfriend," she said. "You may have saw me with him the last time you were here."
"What's your name?" Midget asked, cutting his eyes at her Golden legs.
"Christine, but everybody call me Crystal

Goodhead."

"What should I call you?"

"Excuse me," the security detail said to Midget. "You gotta come from behind there."

"He's with me Sowende," said Crystal.

"Did you let Benny and Micheal know?"

"I haven't seen them; but when I…"

"Come on," Midget interjected, politely directing her to the dance floor.

They started grinding to Keith Sweat's "There's A Right and A Wrong Way to Love Somebody." Her face, breasts and booty were all so soft. Midget had his way with the young, sack-chasing gold-digger. He squeezed her panty-less ass while breathing futuristic lies in her ear. Tightening her arms around Midget's waist, Crystal pressed her pelvis into his throbbing penis. He leaned his head back. As their eyes met in mutual attraction, Nancy walked up.

"Excuse me!" she said, pealing Crystal off Midget.

"Don't put your damn hands on me," Crystal barked, pulling her skirt down.

"Little girl, please," Nancy said as she walked away holding Midget's hand.

Crystal stood there looking lost until Tyree slid up on her and did what he wanted.

"I'm ready to go," said Nancy.

"Didn't you say Bernadette was supposed to be…"

"That bitch probably somewhere looking at some nigga's ceiling."

"You wanna look at my ceilin?" he cracked.

"Are you going to give me a reason to look at your ceiling?"

"All night," he replied, grabbing his crotch.

"Please. I'm talking about that," she said, pinching his lips.

"What?!"

Nancy busted out laughing, wasting some of her drink on Midget's white leather pants.

"I'm sorry," she giggled as she used her napk wipe his pants.

"What's this?" she asked, filling her hand with his bulge.

"It's yours."

"Uhm," she sounded, sucking the last of her drink through the straw.

"I told you what I want," she grinned.

"You gonna take that ride with me?"

"Are you gonna put that inside for me?" she asked, pointing at his tongue.

"Stop playin' Nana."

"I ain't playin.'"

"You know I don't do nothin' like that."

"Well..."

"I need you," he pleaded, kissing her on the face.

"I got needs too."

"I can satisfy all that with this," he replied, placing her hand on his dick.

"Now you really need to stop playing," she laughed.

"Whatchu tryin' to say?!"
Nancy gazed into his eyes.
"You so funny," she said. "I don't know why I love you so much."
"This is why!" Midget grabbed his crotch with both hands.
"How much of that is the leather pants and how much is yours?"
"Whatchu gonna do, that's all I need to know?"
"Eat my pussy and I'll go."
"Do what?!" he snapped.
She laughed so loud, that everyone across from them turned around and smiling as if they knew what was going on.
"I don't do no shit like that !" he growled.
"Well, let Myeesha carry it back for you."
Tyree and Crystal slid out of the door. Seymour was still sitting in his car. Link was in his office doing what Link always did as the club continued to bounce.
"You know Myeesha don't..."
"Nope," she interrupted.
"You the only one I trust Nana."
"It's always Nana when you want some ass or want me to do something"
"I'ma take care of you."
"Are you gonna eat it?"
"Why you doing this to me?"
"You tryin' to come up, right?"
"Yeah, baby."

"Well you gotta go down first."

"I can't believe this shit!"

Nancy smirked as she ordered another drink. Midget looked at her like he wanted to beat her ass.

"You want something to drink?" she asked with laughter.

"You know damn well I don't drink!"

"I was just being nice," she said drawling. "You don't have to get so hy-style"

"Don't play with me, Nancy."

"Don't play with me, Nancy," she mimicked, while perking his lips.

"You gonna do that for me?" he asked sadly.

"Are you gonna eat my…"

"I don't know how," he interjected.

"I'll teach you."

"Fuck you!"

Midget walked away steaming mad with Nancy following behind.

He stood outside the club looking around for Tyree. Nancy stood beside him with a plastic cup in her hand humming along with Freddie Jackson's song, "Rock Me, Tonight." Midget cut his eye at her. She laughed so hard, she shot her drink through her nose.

"That's good for you," he said. "You shoulda choked."

He walked the parking lot looking for Tyree's bomb.

"Here he come!" Nancy shouted.

Midget walked back past the black Saab with the

dark-tinted windows parked next to the white limousine.

Kim's head popped up. She peeped out of the window and then dropped her head back between Seymour's legs. Crystal kissed Tyree on the face and stuck a stick of double-mint in her mouth. She strutted past Nancy, rolling her eyes. Nancy laughed and got in the backseat of the bomb with Midget. Again, Kim popped up. This time her mouth was filled with Seymour's semen. He shot a sinister grin at her, filling her hand with small rocks of crack. Satisfied with her payment, she jumped from his car and disappeared the night. Seymour left for uptown to change cars and to meet with Freddie B. and Kalvin G, two stick up kids who hated Midget Molley as much as he did.

Link was walking out of his office with Jackie, a tall, thick, dark-skinned woman with short hair, when Crystal spotted him.

"Where you been?!" she barked.

Jackie brushed the remaining coke off her vacuum-nose and strolled through the hallway.

"I was taking care of some business," said Link, kissing Crystal on the lips.

"Are we still going to Diamond's after-party?" she asked

"Why?"

"I'm tired."

"I want you to come with me," he said, pulling her close.

"For what?"

"So we can all..."

Link whispered the rest in her ear.

"You must've sniffed too much coke because I'm not doing that!" she swore.

"You wanna have my baby, don't you?"

"Yeah," she said. "Is that guy Midget Molley gonna be there?"

"You met him?"

"Uh-huh."

"Where he at?"

"I just seen him outside with some skeezah, Do you know him too?"

"Everybody know him," Link said, walking her upstairs.

"Why you taking me up here with all these old farts?"

"Thirty ain't old."

"It is to me, I like it downstairs."

"I need to talk to Miss D."

"She up here?"

"She been up here! Whose limo you think that is outside."

"Midget's."

Link laughed so hard he tripped on the carpet.

"You see that leather suit he had on?" he asked laughingly.

"It looked nice to me," said Crystal

"That old ass shit?" he continued, laughing,

"I m going back downstairs."
"Come speak to Miss D. first."
"Soon you gonna want me to eat with her."
"Sleep with her too," he laughed.
"You really been sniffing too much of that shit if you think I'ma sleep with another bitch!"
"Yo, Diamond," Link hollered.
She held up her hand and whispered something to the woman sitting next to her.
"What's up, Link Lover Boy?" asked Miss D..
"A little blow and she'll lick you dry," he said.
"You know Jackie?"
"Do I?!"
"Oh, really?"
"I had her in my office for..."
"I'm taking her home with me," said Ms. D. "I hope your little high maintenance mama don't mind us three having some fun tonight."

Link called Crystal over from the huge picture-window facing the bay. The lights from the Castle Casino danced across the small body of water splashing against the Yacht Club docks. Crystal was held spellbound by the spectacular view. Catching her distant state, Link walked over and turned her towards him.
"What's wrong, baby?" he asked.
"Nothing," she said, holding back her tears.
"Come speak to Miss D."
"I'll be over there."
Crystal was having second thoughts about her plot

with Seymour.

"Get it together girl," she said to herself.

Inhaling deeply, she dried her eyes and joined Link at Diamond's table.

"Hi Diamond."

"Hey Crystal, It's beautiful scenery out there huh?"

"Uh-huh."

"What's wrong? You seem a little down."

"She don't like it up here," said Link.

"Is that right?" asked Diamond, reaching for Crystal's waist. "When you gonna let me take you to the top of the Castle and treat you nice?"

"She cost a lot of money," said Link, smiling.

"I gotta lot of money, And it's good too."

"So is this," said Crystal, lifting her skirt exposing her black butterfly thong. "But you'll never find out."

She walked down the stairs. Link just laughed as Miss D bit her bottom lip. She wanted Crystal, and she wanted her bad.

Chapter 5
FAKE IT TIL YOU MAKE IT

Tyree dropped off Midget and Nancy at the Flagship Hotel on Maine Avenue. There was a black and gold ninja motorcycle parked out front.

"What is he doing here?" Nancy hissed.

"Who?"

"That's Nasheed's bike."

That name rang a bell to Midget. They walked into the lobby.

"Is he from Bacharach?" Midget asked.

"Uh-huh, And I'm telling his..."

A dark-skinned guy with a tapered fade walked off the elevator with a short female with a honey-brown complexion.

"Hi Marneta; Hi Khaleef."

"Hey, girl. What you doing here?" Marneta asked.

"I need to be asking you that," said Nancy.

They both smiled.

"I thought that was Nasheed's bike. I was going to tell his wife as soon as I saw her."

"You still crazy," she said.

"Who's that?"

The Myth of Midget Molley   Ali Rob

She pointed to the check-in desk.

"My sorry-ass friend."

"Friend?!" asked Marneta skeptically slanting her head with raised eyebrows.

"He is," said Nancy smiling.

"Where he from?"

"Here!"

"A.C.?!"

"Girl, stop playing! That's Midget Molley."

"Ohmigod! You know him?!"

"Bye, Marneta."

"Hold up," she pleaded.

Khaleef walked over.

"That's the guy Nasheed was telling you about," Marneta said to Khaleef as Midget and Nancy walked onto the elevator.

"What guy?" he asked, pushing the huge glass doors open.

"Midget Molley!"

"Where?!"

"That was him at the front desk when you were standing there."

"I thought I heard the lady say Molley or something."

"Oh my god," said Marneta. "I can't believe I saw him."

The motorcycle's engine rumbled. Khaleef turned the throttle, revving the motor. Marneta wrapped her arms around his waist. He looked both ways for traffic. There was none. The 1200cc roared away.

An hour passed with Midget putting in extra work on Nancy. He was trying to dick her into submission. He sweated profusely. Violently, the bed shook against the wall. Nancy moaned. Her legs spread wide open. Midget fell deeper into her pulsating pussy, powerfully pushing his penis past her pelvis. They fucked wildly. Nancy screamed, releasing an intense orgasm. Then he exploded his load.

At the same moment the door to Diamond's Westside home flew open. The force from Kalvin's 300 lb body pushing through knocked Candace to the floor.

Seymour entered behind Kalvin and ran up the stairs. Freddie B. snatched the pistol-grip AK-47 from under his coat. He ran through the dining room and kitchen, forcing the negligee wearing, coke sniffing SGTO crew into the living-room. The scene was chaotic as party music continued to blare through the house. Candy cut a sharp eye at Candace's bleeding forehead. Their guns were in reach but the robbers had them all piled together. Kalvin locked the door and whispered in Freddie's ear.

"Put 'em in the closet," he said.

Pulling and kicking them in that direction, Freddie barked at the girls to get into the closet.

"Not you!" Kalvin G. growled.

He dragged Candy by the hair into the dining room, ripping her red teddy from her bronze-colored body.

Upstairs, Miss D's long, wet tongue danced all over Crystal's coke-covered cunt. Link laid to the left, while

The Myth of Midget Molley   Ali Rob

Jackie licked his coke draped dick.

Crystal climaxed in Miss D's face and headed to the bathroom. As she moved down the hall, she ran right into Seymour. He yoked her and whispered in her ear. Miss D. strapped on her favorite dildo, the big black one, and slid every inch inside Jackie. Just as Jackie gasped, Seymour kicked the door open. Startled by the sudden commotion, Miss D. looked over her shoulder in time to see a flash of fire cutting through the dimly lit room. An instant later, the .32 caliber round pieced her eye, blowing her brains out the back of her head.

Watching Ms. D's lifeless body fall to the ground, Jackie screamed for help. Seymour blasted another round, silencing her pleas.

Link jumped up to rush Seymour, but he was too late. Another round hit the upper-part of his chest. He kept charging but fell to the ground, mortally wounded.

Crystal waited for the shooting to stop, then came back from the bathroom. Seymour kept scanning the room like a predator. He spotted a head at the door. He aimed the gun.

"No!" Crystal screamed.

"Where they keep the money?!"

"In the closet."

Nervously she walked towards Link.

His eyes were up in his head. His hand was shaking. As she turned to walk away, his arm moved, touching her leg.

"Aahh!" she yelled.

Seymour flew from the walk-in closet, shooting Link in the head. The force from the round spattered blood on Crystal's face. She was shaken. A stick up was something she was always down for, but she'd never done anything this grimey. Her eyes welled up as she watched brain matter ooooze from the hole in Link's head.

"Where Midget?!" Seymour snapped insanely looking around the room.

"He didn't get here yet."

"Is this all the money?"

"Yeah, I think so."

"Damn! Where the shit?!"

"She keep it hidden in the closet floor downstairs."

"Get dressed!" Seymour barked.

"Help me put Link's clothes on," said Crystal.

"For what?!"

"So we can put him in his car and make it look like..."

"Bitch!"

A loud gun-blast followed.

The music thumped from the yellow Porsche as it pulled in front of the house.

"Kalvin," Freddie B. whispered. "There's a car out front."

Frustrated, Bertha banged on the steering wheel. There was no where to park. Kalvin G. busted a load in Patra like he did with Candy, Candace and Pasha.

The Myth of Midget Molley   Ali Rob

Bertha knew something wasn't right. Putting the car in reverse, she backed it down the street. She parked behind the black Impala and waited. From where she'd posted, Bertha saw the lights go out in the bedroom facing the street. Next the living room lights went out. She decided move in for a closer look. Her heart raced with fear as she walked by the sycamore tree along the side of the house.

Suddenly, the door came open. Bertha ducked behind the bushes with her gun tightly in hand. The same party music played on as the three cold-blooded murderers walked out. Bertha shook with fear. A moaning sound came from upstairs but it was drowned out by the music. She waited for the men to get in the black Impala and drive off. She didn't know what to do. There was something eerie about the house.

"I'll call," she thought to herself, *running to her Porsche.*

As Ms. D's phone kept ringing, tears fell from Bertha's eyes. Slowly driving away from the house, she made an anonymous call to 911.

By 6:30 a.m. the massacre had become a major news story.

"Riiing," Myeesha's phone loudly blared out.

"Hello," she answered groggily.

"Get up!" Diane shouted.

"Girl, I am too tired for..."

"No, girl! Turn the TV on! Hurry up!"

"What's wrong?" Myeesha asked, jumping from the

bed towards the small set on the dresser. "What channel?"

"Channel two and hurry up!" Diane shouted. "Somebody killed all those. people."

"Ohmigod!" screamed Myeesha at the image of Miss D's limousine surrounded by yellow police tape. "Where's Midget!"

Across town back at the hotel, Midget and Nancy were walking to the elevator to check out when he noticed Bertha going into one of the rooms.

"Don't let Miss D. catch you," he smiled.

Too dazed to respond, she stared ahead of her.

"You see that?" he asked Nancy.

"All those bitches are weird," she said.

The elevator opened and Khaleef and Marneta stepped off.

"You heard what happened?!"

"What?" Nancy asked as Midget held the elevator.

"Somebody killed Miss D," said Marneta. "They got helicopters all over the place."

Midget's heart flew into his throat. His eyes widened with disbelief.

"Let's go, Nancy!" he said with a sense of urgency.

"See you girl," said Nancy. "You be careful."

"You too," replied Marneta.

As soon as the elevator doors opened to the main floor, Midget rushed to the front desk and had the attendant ring Bertha's room. He let it ring countless times, but nobody answered. Bertha just laid there crying at the television as an Action News reporter gave the gruesome account.

"*Eight people now lay dead and another hospitalized when what started out as a festive affair turned into multiple homicide,*" said the reporter. "*The best way to describe the scene in the Westside home, owned by Diamond Dewitt, is cold-blooded murder.*"

Meanwhile, Myeesha had been driving up and down the Strip and around K-Y desperately looking for Midget. Giving up, she nearly hit a taxicab as she sped down Baltic Avenue to Diane's.

That same taxi parked down the street from Stanley Holmes.

Midget reached over and kissed Nancy.

"I gotta pick that up by Sunday," he whispered. "Are you gonna go with me."

"Are you gonna do what I ask you?"

"Come on Nancy," he pleaded "I can't do that."

"Well I can't carry it back for you."

The fat, black, nosey cab driver snickered to himself.

Midget turned his body sideways and pleaded.

"Please baby."

Nancy laughed at Midget's discomfort as the cab driver adjusted his rearview mirror to bear witness.

"It's just this one time Nana, Please."

"That's what I asked you last night."

"But I can't eat no pussy Nancy!"

"Yeah, well I can't carry no…"

"A-hem," grunted the nosy cab driver, sarcastically clearing his throat.

Midget got the message. He handed Nancy a twenty dollar bill. She just looked at it. Digging back in his pocket, he pealed off four more and said, "I'll call you."

"Whatever," she mumbled.

Phones all over the city rang like crazy. Wanda rushed out of the shower and answered hers.

"Who is this?!" she demanded, her body shivering from the central air blowing through her townhouse apartment.

"It's me, Wanda," said the elderly voice.

"Oh I'm sorry Granny, I was getting ready for work."

"Well I didn't mean to call so..."

"Can you hold on for a second?" Wanda asked. "Someone's buzzing the other line."

"Crystal's been shot; that's why I..."

"Huh?!"

"Yes. Someone killed..."

"Ohmigod!"

"I'm too old for..."

"Where?"

"The police called here and said I need to get to the hospital."

"Jesus!" exclaimed Wanda.

"My caretaker's not here and..."

"Who was she last with?"

"Lord. I don't know. I raised that child all by myself.

She just wouldn't listen to me. I'm tired," said the elderly woman. "This stuff been on the news all morn..."

Wanda dropped the phone on the bed and ran downstairs. She clicked the television on and grabbed the living-room phone.

"Granny!" she shouted.

"Yes, child."

"What channel?"

"The local one."

Wanda pressed channel two with the remote control.

"*...One thing that's clear, Chirstine Goodhead is very lucky to be alive this morning,*" intoned the reporter.

"I need you to go down there 'cause I'm too old for this. I have no way of ..." continued the despondent grandmother.

"I'll..."

"They called here asking me all kinds of questions, I don't know that child's business. I'm 75-years old and..."

Her voice went silent as if caught up with sadness and disappointment.

"I'll go down there Granny, Please don't worry yourself."

"That child's killing me Wanda," said Ms. Jackson, now choked up. "They say she in critical..."

"Don't cry Granny, She'll be alright."

"Lord, I'm too old for this," she wept. "I begged that poor child..."

"Please Granny, She'll make it."

"Jesus know I can't live without that child, I'm too old for..."

"She'll be fine," Wanda said. "I love you."

"Please come see me."

"I will, I'll be there after I come from the hospital."

"Okay. Thank you baby, Thank you so much."

"You don't have to thank me Granny," said Wanda. "I love you and I love Crystal's like a sister, You just rest up."

The city was a virtual ringing bell. Phones were jumping off the hook.

AZ called Ali, Jihad called Akeem, AB called Lil Bilal, Barkim called Little Mansfield and Midget called Big Lou.

"Hello."

"Is Louie there?"

"No he's not, Who's calling?"

"Midget."

"Hey, stranger!"

"Who dis?!"

"Delora."

"Hey, Dee. What's up?!"

"Nothing much."

Delora was Big Lou's mistress. She was voluptuous, vivacious and virile. She had to be. She'd controlled all the heroin that flowed on her block in the 70's.

"Where Louie?" Midget asked.

"He had to run out for a second but he left that here for you."

The Myth of Midget Molley   Ali Rob

"I'ma try to get up there tomorrow," said Midget. "I'm waiting on Nancy."

"How she doing?"

"She alright," he said. "Just giving me a hard time about comin' up there to pick it up."

"Why?"

"You know how she can be," replied Midget. "Plus somebody killed the girl that had all the Boy down here."

"I know you not talking about little Diamond!"

"You know Miss D?!"

"Yeah, she's from Saint Anne's!" Delora shouted. "George was supplying her before he got busted! What happened?"

"Somebody murdered everybody in her house."

"Louie said she may've been working with the feds."

"What?!"

"That's exactly what I said."

"That's crazy!"

"But you know how the streets talk."

"She was well liked down here."

"I hope George didn't have her killed."

"It's hard to say whether it was a hit or robbery but they murdered everybody for a reason," said Midget. "If it was a hit they could've got her in the street and if it was a simple robbery they could have just taken the money and left. It's just hard to say."

"I know," said Delora. "She couldn't have had that much product 'cause the feds hit George a few months ago and I know she wouldn't fuck with no one else."

"I don't know" he said. "Everybody's on edge."

"I don't blame 'em."

"They never had nothin' like that happen down here."

"Yeah, well that type of shit is always happening in the Bronx," said Delora. "Shit's changed since the 70's, People are robbing and killing their own friends…"

"Their family too," Midget interjected.

"Let me beep Louie 'cause I know he's not gonna believe this."

"Do he know her like that?"

"He knew her and George since they were kids. Let me go," she said, her voice now shaking.

"Okay," said Midget, "you take care."

Midget placed the kitchen phone on the wall-hook and opened the refrigerator. Just then Myeesha walked in the door. He pulled his head out of the ice-box and was smothered by her relieved embrace.

From a safe haven in Philly, Mia made a call back to the City.

"Hello," answered a sleepy voice.

"Where Pam?!"

"Who is this?!"

"It's me Ms. Martin."

"Who the hell is me?!"

"Mia."

"Well don't you know how to speak before you start asking for someone?!"

The Myth of Midget Molley   Ali Rob

"Yes ma'am."
"Pam don't pay no damn bills here!"
Mia didn't say a word.
Throwing the phone on the bed, Ms. Martin dragged herself to Pam's room.
"Pam!" she shouted.
"Whaaaat?" drawled Pam, pulling the sheets over her head.
"This damn child want you on the phone."
"Whoooo?"
"Get the hell up and find out dammit!" said her mother. "You need to get a damn job!"
"Make me sick," Pam mumbled as Ms. Martin walked out.
"Hello," she uttered from under the sheets..
"Pam! Get up!"
"Mia!" she yelled, jumping up.
"Yeah, girl! somebody..."
"Where the hell you been?!" Pam interjected.
"In Philly," she said. "Somebody killed Miss D."
"Huh?!"
"Yeah, girl. Somebody killed her, the twins and..."
"Ohmigod!" she screamed.
Her mother ran into the room.
"What's wrong?!" Ms. Martin asked.
"Sombody..."
Pam couldn't finish. Grief stricken, she fell in her mother's arms crying.
Ms. Martin grabbed the phone and asked Mia what

happened.

"It's all on ACTION NEWS that somebody killed a bunch of people."

"A bunch of people where?!"

"Out there in Atlantic City!"

"Do what?!"

Ms. Martin placed Pam's head on the pillow and turned the television to channel six. Pam sobbed as the helicopters flew over the house on Monroe Drive, and some unconcerned-seeming white man reported the names of the deceased. Ms. Martin put the phone on the hook and shook her head in the disgust.

After Mia hung up, AJ walked over and kissed away her tears just as their phone rang.

Mia looked at him in shock.

"Who have this number?" she sobbed.

"Go head upstairs and get dressed, and pack your stuff too," he said, picking up the phone.

"Yo!" he answered.

"I took care of that," said the caller.

"Yeah, I seen it on the news."

"I'll be in the School House when you get wn."

"Okay."

AJ smiled and headed up the steps.

Seymour walked back into his bedroom in his grandmother's house. Freddie B. and Kalvin G. had just finished counting the money.

"Yo!" Freddie B. growled. "I thought you said this bitch had millions! Ain't shit here but two hundred thousand dollars!"

"How we gonna split that?" Kalvin G. barked.

"Hold up," said Seymour. "It's suppose to be more than..."

His grandmother knocked on the door. Seymour motioned for them to keep quiet as he turned and walked out of the door.

"Yo, I-Kee! This nigga lied to us." Freddie snarled. "Where he put the guns?"

"Look in the closet!" he said. "That nigga knew she didn't have no million dollars in that house."

"The guns ain't..."

Seymour walked back into the room.

"Yo. Link use to tell Crystal that Miss D. was sittin' on millions," said Seymour.

"That don't mean she had millions," said Freddie B. "This ain't even bail money!"

"Yo I-Kee, y'all can have the money," Seymour said. "Just give me the product."

"Bet!" said Kalvin G.

"Fuck that! Give us half the product too," said Freddie B. "We got five bodies on our hands.

"How many you think I got!" Seymour said as he backed up and got in position.

"I don't know what the fuck your motive was!" said Freddie B. jumping up. "Why we had to kill everybody! And what about Midget? I thought you said he was gonna be there."

"Yo. I'm tellin' you man, You better stop actin' like..."

"Man, fuck you!"

Kalvin leaped to his feet, moving between them.

"Yo. Take the shit!" Seymour roared, throwing the half kilo of heroin in Freddie B's chest.

"No!" Kalvin G. said. "Let's split it."

"Fuck that! If he don't want none, don't beg his ass."

"Just call us a cab man."

Seymour cut his lazy eye nefariously at Freddie B. and smiled as he got up to make the call.

Myeesha laid next to Midget listening to everything he said. She was tired of arguing and fighting with him. She loved him unconditionally and only wanted to spend the rest of her life with him. She surrendered.

"I'ma give you five thousand dollars to lease a Condo in Pleasantville," said Midget. "Pay three months in advance and get the phones cut on. I have to get you and the children out of this City."

"I told you these guys were out here robbing and..."

"It's alright baby." Midget said. "Just pack everything and rent a U-Haul as soon as you secure a new place."

"Honey, promise me nothing will happen to you."

"Nothing will happen."

"How can you be sure?"

"I can't but..."

"You can't?!" she echoed.

"Please don't start cryin'."

"I can't live without you," said Myeesha, wrapping

The Myth of Midget Molley   Ali Rob

her arms around him.

"I got this!" said Midget. "This is what I do!"

"But what if the same people that killed Miss D. come after you?"

"I'ma handle my business!"

"But what if..."

"I'm good at what I do, so don't worry about that."

"You going to stop as soon as you get enough money to buy us a house and..."

"As soon as I buy you a big home and a brand new car, I'm outta there."

"Promise?"

"I promise," he said, as he opened her gown and began mouthing her breasts.

Exhaling, she laid back. Midget made love to Myeesha like he'd done a year before when he first gotten out of prison. She loved it. The pot-washing job was history. Midget Molley was back in the game.

Back at Seymour's, the cab driver blew the horn repeatedly. Kalvin G. and Seymour shook hands and embraced warmly. Freddie B. gritted at him.

The three walked out on the porch.

"Yo! Don't forget what I told you," Seymour said. "Lay low. Don't start splurgin' until shit cool down."

A thin man in a navy-blue sweats and a baseball cap pulled down just past his brow rode by on a bicycle. Freddie and Kalvin G hopped in the cab and sped off.

The cab stopped at the red light on the corner of

Rhode Island and Madison Avenues. Freddie B. and Kalvin G. never saw it coming. The cab driver did but it was too late. The man on the bike was Yunus.

Jumping off, Yunus ran to the cab and dumped a .357-python round into Freddie's head. Kalvin G. turned in panic to reach for the door. Snatching the other door open, Yunus reached over and shot him in the back of the head. Instinctively, he shot the cab driver too. Grabbing the black gym bag, he hopped back on the bike and rode off in the opposite direction.

Seymour was making his mark and Atlantic City was becoming all the more violent. Midget knew this too.

"Honey," Myeesha said. "I don't want to ever lose you."

"You not gonna lose me," said Midget. "I just want you and the children out of this city before it explode. Somebody is tryin' to send a message."

"A message?"

"Yeah."

"To who?" she asked, sitting up in the bed.

"I don't know," he said, laying her head on his chest."

"Do you think the mafia did it?"

"Nah."

"Why would someone kill Miss D.? Everyone liked her, Link too."

"I don't know."

"Honey," Myeesha whispered.

The Myth of Midget Molley   Ali Rob

"Yes."
"I love you."
"I love you too darling."
"Tell me I'll never have to spend many nights without you."
"You won't."
"Tell me no one will hurt you."
"I'm Midget Molley!"
"So!" Myeesha said, lifting her head from his chest. "They killed Miss D and she was the..."
"I'm not Miss D?"
"But..."
"No. Miss D thought she was loved, I know I'm not loved."
"I love you."
"I'm not talkin' 'bout you."
"The kids love you, My family love you, Your family love you..."
"I'm talkin' 'bout the streets! There's no such thing as love in the drug game."
"But you said you love the game."
"I love the excitement of the game."
"But without the people there's no game and without the game there's no excitement," said Myeesha.
"You right. But the people I'm talkin 'bout are the ones who be hatin' just because somebody gettin' paid and they not."
"Do you think that's who killed Miss D.?"
"If I was a gambling man, I bet dollars to donuts

Tareek and Denny did that shit."

"But why would they kill everybody?"

"Listen Honey," said Midget, moving her head off his chest. "If a person rob me they'll kill me, It's as simple as that."

"Why?"

"Because they know if they let me live, I'ma kill everything, the cat, the dog, the babies, everything!!!"

"Is that the reason why they killed everybody in Miss D. house?"

"That could be a reason if it was a robbery."

"What else could it had been?"

"A hit."

"A hit?" she repeated.

"Yeah, This game is vicious!" he said. "If they had left Miss D and Link alive they' woulda set this city on fire and burnt everybody they even thought had something to do with robbing 'em."

"Do you think the Soul Girls will start..."

"They finished!" he interjected.

"I didn't hear them mention Miss D. sister's name."

"She gotta sister?!"

"Yeah! They say she the one that got all the money."

"Is she part of the SGTO crew?"

"Yeah, I showed her to you at the club that night."

"I don't remember."

"Do you remember that beauty salon?"

"What beauty salon?"

"The one down from where your mom used to live."

"Okay, I know which one you talkin' 'bout," said Midget.

"That's where I use to see those girls going at with those big gym bags."

Their conversation was interrupted by a phone ring. It was Tyree.

Across town at his Grandmother's house Seymour sat on the porch playing with his German-Shepherd dog. Yunus rolled up on the bike. He hopped off and carried the package into the house. Seymour locked the door and the two of them double-stepped up the stairs.

"Here! Get rid of this," Yunus said handing Seymour the python.

"This shit still smokin'," said Seymour laughing.

"That's the real deal!"

"I knew you like it."

"Damn! What were they doing riding around with all this money and product?"

"That's what I got outta the house I was tellin you about."

"You already hit that?!" Yunus asked, spreading the money out on the bed.

"Yeah. I couldn't put it off until Sunday," said Seymour. "I took those two dumb muthafuckas because the bitch that set it all up was gonna let them do it if I didn't hit last night."

"How much she get?"

"Now when did I start givin' a bitch anything but a

mouthful of cum and a..."

"That's all she wanted?!" Yunus interjected.

"That and what I gave her."

"What's that?"

"One to the head," he said, holding his hand like a gun.

"Did you know them dudes?"

"Who?"

"The ones in the cab?"

"Hell no! They some dumb mothafuckas! They started raping those
freaks and stickin shit inside their..."

"No protection?"

"I-Kee, them chumps didn't even have on gloves."

"What?!"

"Word is bond!"

"They didn't know about DNA?"

"DNA?!" Seymour echoed. "Them suckas didn't know about shit! That's why I called you. I couldn't let them live with that kind of info."

"How we gonna do this?" Yunus asked, separating each one-thousand-dollar bundle, tightly wrapped in rubberbands.

"What? The split?"

"Yeah."

"That's you there," said Seymour, pushing all the loot in one pile.

"Word?!"

"Word is bond! You my peoples, man!"

The Myth of Midget Molley · Ali Rob

"Yo !" said Yunus jumping up to hug his partner in crime. "I love you, I-Kee!"

"I love you too!"

They'd been friends since the 70's

"Whatchu gonna do with that?" said Yunus as he pointed at the half kilo....Hyleema began crying out of control.

"You don't have to cry Sweetie, Daddy love you," said Midget.

"You can cry all you want," said Myeesha, raising the knife up.

"Come on, stab me Bitch!" growled Midget, walking towards her.

"Move Hyleemah," she shouted, pushing her daughter out of the way. "This mothafucka think I won't kill his black ass!"

"I'ma step on it, break it down into bundles and pass it out to my little workers."

"You don't need a couple of these?"

He offered Seymour two handfuls of money.

"Check this out," he said, opening the closet and sliding a little trap door back. "Stick your head in there and look at that."

"Damn!"

Yunus saw stacks of money and at least ten different hand guns and five assault weapons.

"What the fuck is this?"

"A Desert Eagle."

"Let me get this when I come home?"

"It's yours man."

"Damn, this motha fucka 'a make a nigga shit on his self!"

"Give it here, Let me put it back up."

"I gotta get back to the crib," said Yunus. "I'ma holla at my people as soon as I get to the spot."

"Yeah man, holla at him because dude trippin 'bout that bitch."

"I gotchu."

"Yo I-Kee, you gotta get right on top of..."

"I gotchu, Just chill-out."

"I'm sayin, I-Kee, he keep disrespectin' me and..."

"What I say?"

"Alright now. If I..."

"What?"

"If he keep..."

"Ah shut up!" said Yunus, throwing a pillow at him.

Seymour dove on Yunus and they started play wrestling when Seymour's .9mm fell from his waist and went off just missing Yunus' feet. They both laughed and play fought for the gun. Yunus got it and jumped to his feet.

"You know what it is, nigga!" he growled, pointing the gun at his main man. "You seen it before! Now get on the floor!"

The two of them busted out laughing, remembering how they'd said the same words to John P. when they robbed him and stuffed him in the closet.

The Myth of Midget Molley   Ali Rob

"Yo. I gotta finish breakin' the joints down we used on the thing last night and the one you just used," said Seymour. "Then I'ma shoot to the School House.

"Okay. I'ma lay low at my wife's spot."

"When you gettin out for good?"

"Around December," said Yunus. "Why?"

"I got this other dude I wanna hit."

"Who?"

"Aaron."

"Aaron?!" he replied, a bit surprised.

"Yeah. They call him AJ."

"Little short AJ that think he's a player?!"

"Yeah." Seymour laughed.

"You can't fuck with little AJ," said Yunus.

"Why?"

"I'm just sayin…"

"Money is money," said Seymour coldly. "You know how it go."

"Yeah Ahk, but there's a few others you can hit besides Lil. AJ."

"Aheem and Akeel?"

"Now that's who you should get, not AJ."

"I know but I'm about that paper."

"They doin' a little somethin'."

"We'll see what happen," said Seymour. "All I need you to do is holla at Midget."

"He ain't thinkin 'bout you!"

"I know but every time he see my little workers gettin' with Kim, he snap."

"Make her disappear!"

"I told you before," said Seymour, "he gonna blame me."

"Well make her O.D."

"He'll blame me for that too, He crazy 'bout that bitch!"

"Just take her ass to a base house and let her smoke 'til her heart bust! Remember how Benton did those two freaks at his crib!"

"Oh yeah!"

"Just like that…"

"But I'm tellin' you I-Kee, if he step to me one more time about that ho…."

"Yahda, Yahda, Yahda," Yunus mocked. "How long y'all been beefin'?

"Yeah, but I'm serious now," said Seymour.

"Yeah I know, Holla at me before I go back."

Yunus left Seymour's grandmother's house with the gym bag over his shoulder. Instead of calling a cab, he walked around the corner and jumped on a jitney at New Hampshire Avenue and got off at Iowa Avenue, down from the Golden Nugget casino. He waved a taxi down and had it drop him off at his wife's house. Seymour went downtown a totally different way. He drove his brand new 1986 Saab down Vermont Avenue until he got to Atlantic Avenue. He made a right turn and headed to the School House Apartments.

Just as Seymour parked, Tyree arrived at Midget's house. Myeesha had already left. They rode down the

The Myth of Midget Molley   Ali Rob

Strip in Tyree's bomb checking out the scenery. With no hustlers to be seen, all the fiends ran up to the car complaining to Midget there was nothing on the block. They wouldn't stop pouring rumors in his ears until he shooed them away with a few dollars. But that didn't stop Betty, the base head, from hanging onto the door handle. She pleaded with Midget to listen to her.

Somebody said Miss D. was killed to send a warning to you," said Betty.

"To me," he smiled.

"That's what they said."

"Who?"

"Somebody said the BMC Boys started a 'Clean-Up-the-Community' campaign."

"A what?!" Tyree asked.

"Citizens Rallying Against Criminals & Kingpins," said Betty, handing Midget a leaflet.

"Let me see that!"

"Hold up!" said Midget. "I know these punks ain't startin' that shit again!"

"Let me see it!" Tyree insisted.

Midget handed it to his main man and gave Betty a $20 dollar bill.

"Thanks," she said, running towards Carver Hall.

"I bet those punks killed that broad," said Tyree, balling up the paper.

"Man fuck those niggas!" said Midget, as he headed toward K-Y and the Curb. "We takin' these streets, What the fuck is the Crack Coalition?"

When they arrived at K-Y and the Curb the scene was the same as the Strip, plenty of fiends looking to buy, but very few hustlers selling. The frustrated fiends fought furiously for the few bags of heroin and vials of crack the weekend dealers were selling. Weekend dealers were the 9-to-5 hustlers, the ones who worked real jobs but hustled on the block during the weekends. The deaths of Link and Miss D left a major void, but the big boys with the weight were scared to step in and fill it. The city was primed for a real take over.

As soon as Tyree pulled onto Gino's parking lot, the addicts there rushed Midget, thinking he had the package. They wanted that rock. Heroin was slowly fading out. Cocaine was fast becoming king. Aiming to please his customers, Midget promised he'd soon deliver.

From Gino's, he walked over to Sapp's Luncheonette. The tall dark-skinned man with the fat face sat at the rear of the eatery spooning Sapp's famous bean soup into his mouth. Midget strolled to the back and sat in the old man's booth. Stacey, the 40ish woman living with the old, blind man, brought Midget a bowl of bean soup.

"Thanks," he said with a smile

"Kill Seymour," the blind man said between spoonfuls of soup.

Midget's eyes widened. His heart pounded.

"Now?" he asked, feeling startled about the bleak order from his old man.

"Now, tomorrow, next week, whenever but not later

than..."

The door chimed as it came open. Midget's head flew over his shoulder.

"Hi, Tyree!" said Stacey, raising her voice.

The door chimed open again. Jeanie, Patsy and Vikki walked in. Stacey spoke to all of them by name, the same as she did whenever anyone came in. This was the system to alert Mr. Kirkland who was there. When she didn't know them by name, which was rare, she'd say, *"Hi stranger, how can I help you?"*

Midget raised his index finger, signaling to Tyree he'd be there in a minute.

"Seymour's been robbing people for too long," said the old man.

"He killed all those kids over there on Westside and..."

"Seymour did that?!" Midget emoted in a hushed voice.

"This boy's become a loose cannon," said the mentor. "And if you don't take him out he's gonna take you out."

"I'll blow his fuckin..."

"Calm down Little Caesar; You have to out-think him, set a trap for him."

"So that's who robbed Miss D?"

"It wasn't about robbery, although she was robbed."

"What was it about?!"

"Chess," said the old, blind man, placing a spoon of soup in his mouth.

"Chess?" Midget replied, twisting his face to a confused look.

"Yeah Caesar, he's clearing the streets."

"For who?"

"Not for you," he replied. "If you don't stop him soon, he'll be too strong to bring down."

"No one's too strong to be brought down."

"Don't bet your life on it."

"What's with this Crack Coalition stuff everybody's talkin' 'bout?"

"What did I tell you back in the 70's?"

"About what?"

"About the enemy?"

"You told me a lot of things."

"What I taught you about Shaka Zulu?"

"Oh, I remember."

"What do you remember?" the blind man asked, pushing the empty bowl away."

"When you encounter your enemy, kill him completely."

"And what did I tell you when you came to me about those BMC Boys back in 1980?"

"Kill 'em all!"

"Did you do that?"

"No sir."

"So now they've resurrected themselves under a new name and a new leader."

"Should I make a list?"

The old man laughed and said, "Why not? They got

your name on one."

"I'ma add those two little punks and..."

"Who? My chauffeurs?" he laughed loudly, showing nothing but gums.

"That ain't funny!"

"But it's fun."

"Fun?!" Midget snapped. "What if a car hit you or..."

"Leave them alone," the old man warned.

"Yeah alright," Midget mumbled."

"I see and hear with my ears, remember?"

"Yes sir."

"Leave them alone, You understand?"

"Yes sir."

"And make up your mind whachu gonna do about that girl."

"Who?"

Mr. Kirkland took off his dark shades for the first time since Midget got home from prison. It startled him. The old man's brown eyes were perfect but void of sight. To Midget it was as if the old man was looking right into his eyes, like when he was young.

"Don't ever ask me *who* when you know what I'm talking about," he retorted placing his shades back on.

"I put her in the Program."

"Let her go."

"Huh?"

"Let her go."

"Just walk away?" Midget asked, knowing he couldn't stop caring for Kim.

"You must kill Seymour because of business, not pussy."

"Yeah, he don't have nothin' to do with Kim," Midget agreed, still seeming unsure his own words.

"Just let her go Caesar."

A tear welled in Midget's eye.

"Let her go?" Mr. Kirkland repeated. "It's a whole new world out here. She's not who she used to be. Crack raped her and she fell in love with it."

"What do I do about the SBM?" he asked despondently.

"They're no threat to you,"

"But I heard they into robbin' and..."

"They just some young kids calling themselves the Sons of the Black Mafia," he said. "They're petty little punks robbing prostitutes and out of town pimps. They nothing like the JBM."

"Who that, the man that use to have the walkin' canes?" Midget asked referring to Old Pops who owned the Club Harlem.

"We don't need to talk about that, Bo Diddle will fill you in, Have you went to see him?"

"Nah."

"Why not?"

"I gave them a lot of money and..."

"And they kept the pigs off you."

"Yeah. But Diddle always want money for his time."

"He gonna want money when you start making some, Right now he only want to see you."

"I'll get up there to see him," said Midget. "But what do I do when they ask for contributions?"

"Give them what they ask for," said the blind man, "and they'll give you what you ask for. Fair exchange ain't no robbery."

"But it sure feel like it comin' from them.

"You want to keep the police off you don't you?"

"Yes sir."

"So you pay them for their service, It's just like any other service."

"Okay. I'll go see him."

"And come back to see me after you've talked to him. I'll have all the information you need."

"About what?"

"Where Seymour be."

"I already know where his grandmother stay; Plus he's always out in the street."

"You don't want to get him like that, You need to catch him sleeping.

"His grandmother's house is not good. She's a close friend of Stacey's mother. They all play bingo together. You can't take him out at her house."

"I know how to get his ass."

"Be careful of AJ too," said the old man.

"That's my man!"

"The only man you have is that kid sitting at that table up front there, He'll give his life for you."

"Tyree?" he asked.

"Who else could I be talking about? Get out of here

before I hit you with a right cross."

Midget laughed at his old man throwing a lazy jab into thin air. He stood up, adjusted his pants and kissed Mr. Kirkland like he always did. The door came open as Midget turned to leave.

Seymour walked up to the cashier counter to place his order. Midget turned back to tell the blind man but decided not to say anything. The old man smiled.

"What did you say you wanted?" Stacey asked with a raised voice. "Two big and one small or two small and one big!?"

Seymour was about to answer when he noticed Stacey's eyes shift. He snapped his head to the left catching sight of Midget with his lazy eye. Their eyes locked like two pit bulls facing off. Seymour reached for his gun. Midget just smiled and looked over to his far left. Seymour turned his head just enough to see Tyree's big .44 Magnum aimed directly at him. Shocked, he took a step back and got the hell up outta there.

Tyree laughed and slipped the gun back into his waist.

The two best friends headed up to Pennsylvania and Atlantic Avenues to spend some money at Gene Wallace Men's Clothing Store. They spent twenty-five thousand dollars on suits and shoes. As an old, loyal customer, Midget Molley got served like royalty. *This was where the gangsters went to get their clothes.*

At a bear minimum a suit was $1,000 and a pair of

plain shoes went for half that. Only the fortunate could afford to shop at Gene Wallace and the other hot spot, Tiberius, Midget's next stop.

They strolled into Caesar's Palace taking the escalator up to the second floor where Tiberius Men's Clothing Store was. He ran into Andrew, a childhood friend who worked there.

"What's up with you, Midget?!" Andrew asked. "When you get home?"

"Ain't nothin', I been home for minute now."

"And you just getting up here to see me?"

"Man, I been bustin' my ass just to make ends meet," he said. "It's no way I coulda come here like that."

"Come on man," said Andrew wrapping his arm around Midget, "you know how we do. I'm the manager now. Pick out what you want."

Midget picked up a Versace silk leisure suit in every color. Then he grabbed a dozen pair of linen slacks like the ones Tyree had picked out for himself. They found matching shoes for each outfit they liked. Heading up to the cash register, Tyree opened the handheld leather pouch and reached pay for the merchandise.

"Give that back to him Ebony," said Andrew, handing her his own Platinum Visa card. "Take it out of this."

"Yo. Andrew, I'm straight now, I can..."

"Welcome home," he interjected.

"Thanks man."

"All I ask is, when you do your thing, come in here and spend some of that money."

"You got that!" Midget said, shaking Andrew's hand with appreciation.

They took a taxi to the house. The Gene Wallace van was just pulling up. The young man making the delivery jumped out and slid the side doors open. He followed Midget up the steps into the apartment. He laid the carry bags for each suit on the sofa..

Tyree hopped in the van with his bags and headed to K-Y and the Curb where he'd parked his bomb earlier that day.

At the Flagship Hotel, Seymour pulled his black Saab into the parking garage. He entered the side door leading to the lobby. Walking on to the elevator, he pressed the sixth floor button. The bell chimed, the door opened and he walked right into Bertha.

"Excuse me," he said, rushing to get where he was going.

An evil chill ran through her body from his hand. She cut a sharp eye at him as he walked down the hall. Suddenly her heart experienced a fierce fibrillation.

"That limp," she said to herself.

She began to hyperventilate. Her breast expanded with every breath she took. In a panic, she pressed repeatedly for the elevator to return, hoping Seymour wouldn't come back out.

"Ding."

The elevator door opened. She rushed inside and pressed for the lobby floor with the same urgency.

"Ohmigod!" *she whispered to herself as she wiped the tears away. "That's him."*

The elevator doors opened. Bertha ran towards the huge glass doors and down the concrete steps. She hopped in the Porsche and sped off to Mari's Beauty Salon where Pam, Mia and Mari waited for her.

Seymour sat across from Killer Kurtis and Jazzy Jimmy waiting for AJ to come out of the bathroom. The murderers said nothing to each other until Handsome AJ walked into the bed area dressed in a pair of white linen pants and the hotel's terry-cloth robe.

"Seymour," he said. "This my peoples, Kurt and Jim, they from North Philly. Yo, that's Seymour."

They nodded their heads acknowledging the introduction and continued looking at BET. AJ opened the closet and took out a brown briefcase. Throwing it on the bed, he said, "that's you!"

"How much?" Seymour asked.

"What we agree on?"

"A quarter mil."

"Count it."

"I have no..."

Someone knocked on the door authoritatively. Killer Kurtis and Jazzy Jimmy jumped to their feet with their twin Mac 10s in hand. Seymour simultaneously leaped to his feet with a nickel-plated .45 shining brightly.

"Be cool," AJ whispered as he walked towards the

door. He peered out the peep hole.

"Who the fuck is this?!" he growled, cracking the door.

"Where Seymour?!" the dark-skinned, chinky-eyed woman asked boldly.

"Who the fuck are you?!" AJ growled.

Seymour looked over AJ's shoulder and said, "I be out in a minute, Go wait back in the car."

Kim smacked her lips.

"I wish you hurry up!" she said, walking back towards the elevator.

"I'ma jet man," said Seymour, "Call me if you need me to do somethin' else."

"You know Akeel?" AJ asked.

"Fat Akeel?"

"Yeah."

"I want you to show him to my people."

"I'll take care that for you," Seymour said. "Him and his partner."

"You talking about Aheem?"

"Yeah."

"Just show 'em to my mans, They'll take it from there."

"You want 'em to hangout with me or…"

"That's on you."

"I don't care," said Seymour.

"What y'all wanna do Kurt?" AJ asked.

"Y'all can chill at my spot; My people gettin' ready to move down South," Seymour offered.

"It's cool with me," said Killer Kurtis.
"Me too," said Jazzy Jimmy.
"Let's roll!"
AJ walked the three of them to the door and locked it behind them.

From his apartment Midget sat playing with the new pager that he bought while on the Avenue. The phone rang. It was Myeesha calling to tell him that it'd be a month before they could move into their new unit in the Orchards Condominium Complex in Pleasantville.
"I gave the realtor a month's rent and two months' security," she said.
"Okay."
"Are you gonna be home?" she asked.
"No. I gotta go see Big Lou," said Midget. "Okay, love you."
"I love you too."
"I'll be over Tyeesha's if you need me."
"Alright."
Midget sat for a minute at the kitchen table writing down the names of all the people he could recruit to work for him. Then he wrote down the names of all the young hustlers he planned on selling weight to. Closing his little, black book , he called Nancy,
"Hello."
"Hi baby."
"Hi Midget."
"Whachu doing?"

"Nothing, just sitting here painting my nails."
"For what?!"
"For my man."
"For who?!"
"Boy, stop being so damn jealous." she said. "I'm polishing them for your sorry ass. You gonna lick 'em for me?"
"Do what?!"
She busted out laughing at his response.
"What pleasure can I get outta' lickin' your damn toes?!"
"The pleasure outta fulfilling my needs."
"Yeah well that's a need you just won't get fulfilled. What time you gonna be ready?"
"Ready for what?" Nancy asked.
"To pick that up."
"Pick what up?"
"That package I was telling you about last night."
"Ain't that some shit!"
"What?" Midget asked.
"You want me to carry that shit all the way from New York but..."
"I love you," he interjected.
"Well eat my pussy!"
"What I tell you about that Nancy?"
"And what I tell you about taking me for granted."
"Are you gonna take the ride with me or not?!"
"Are you gonna eat my pussy or not??
"I don't believe this shit!"

The Myth of Midget Molley   Ali Rob

"Excuse me?"
"Why you playin' these fuckin' games?!"
"Who's playing?"
"You!"
"I ain't playing, I want you to eat my pussy."
"This don't make no damn sense."
"It's good too."
"Do what?!" he roared.
She giggled.
"Just do it one time and I'll do that for you."
"I told you I don't know how."
"I'll show you."
"This shit is crazy! This shit is real crazy!"
"Hello, You still there?"
"Nancy, don't make me fuck you up!" Midget threatened.
"I have to go," she said.
"Hold up!"
"No, Because..."
"I'll do it."
"You gonna lick my toes too?"
"Nancy, *psss,* man..."
"Don't come over here with no attitude..."
"I'm not stayin' down there all day."
"Just 'til I cum," she said.
"How long that gonna take?"
"That depends how fast you learn."
"I don't believe this shit!"
"Hmmm, hmmm, hmmm," Nancy hummed.

"What the fuck you humming for?!"
"I told you about cussing at me!"
"Well stop humming in my ear."
"What time you coming over?"
"I'll be there."
"I need to know because..."
"Don't be rushing me!"
"Well don't say nothing if I'm not here when you..."
"I'm comin' now."
"Hurry up because I waited a long time for this."
"This shit don't make no sense."
"Did you say something?"
"Nah," he mumbled sadly. "I'll be there."

Midget was fucked up. In the past he never went through this. He felt it was natural for a woman to have a dick in her mouth but eating pussy was something real gangstas just didn't do. So much had changed since he been gone. Now pussy eating was as common as sucking dick, and the women were asking for head just as boldly as the men had done for ages.

Midget got to The Pitney Village projects on Mississippi Avenue in no time. This was an old hangout of his. He walked through Nancy's door and was stunned to find her sofa lined with four friends. It was as if they were there for a movie. Nancy strolled into the living-room holding a towel against the front of her body. Arlene, her sister Alene, Bernadette and Puerto Rican Rose giggled as Nancy looked at Midget with a devilish grin.

The Myth of Midget Molley   Ali Rob

"What took so long?"

Suddenly feeling embarrassed, he gazed at her with the stare of death.

"I know you heard me talking to you," she said, tauntingly.

Her friends burst into laughter.

"Ain't nothin' funny Bernadette," said Nancy.

They only laughed louder.

"Y'all leave! I'll call y'all when he finish!" she said while showing them to the door.

"I know you didn't tell those bitches my business," he growled after they left.

"Just c'mon eat my pussy," she ordered.

Midget did what he had to do, but when Nancy turned over onto her stomach and asked him to put his face in her ass, he snapped.

She turned back over and said, "Well just keep eating my pussy."

Midget did what he said he'd never do. **Ate that pussy.** Then he went to a motel and spent that night alone. He was too embarrassed to meet Tyree at the club. Instead, he brushed his teeth over and over until he was too tired to do anything else but fall asleep.

The two round-trip tickets to New York sat on the dresser next to his two guns. His eyes slowly closed and he fell into a deep sleep.

While Midget slept, Nancy sat in her living room telling her girls how good Midget could eat pussy.

"My toes curled like this," she said, clenching her

hand into a fist. "He put that long tongue all over my shit and…"

"Did he put his face in it?" Alene asked.

Her sister giggled loudly.

"I grabbed that little head and smeared his eyes, his nose…"

"Stop!" Arlene laughed, rolling over on to the floor.

"Not the gangsta that said he can't do that," Rose chuckled.

"Y'all shoulda seen his face," Nancy laughed, passing the blunt back to Bernadette. "He looked like a baby eating ice-cream."

"Stop it!" Arlene choked with laughter, grabbing her stomach. "I gotta cramp, Stop it!"

"Next time I'ma get that shit on video so I can show it to that bitch; I hate her ass," said Nancy.

"Fuck that Nana, You should call her ass right now," dared Alene.

"Yeah, call her ass," Rose instigated. "Tell that bitch you had her husband eating your shit."

They all busted out laughing as Nancy picked up the phone and dialed Midget's home number.

"Hello," answered Myeesha.

"Shh! It's her, It's her," whispered Nancy to her girls.

"Hello! Who's this?!"

"Don't worry about it, Bitch! Just know that your husband's tongue been all up my ass! Remember that next time he kisses you!"

Click. Nancy hung up the phone. She and her

friends busted out laughing.

"What the fuck?" thought Myeesha, in a state of shock.

Immediately, she grabbed the phone and called Tyeesha.

"Hello."

"Tyeesha, you ain't gonna believe this shit!"

"What is it!?"

Just then the other line clicked.

"Hold on, somebody's on the other line." said Myeesha, before clicking over. "Hello."

"You know who the fuck called you, Bitch!" said Bernadette. "Your man's a pussy-eater. How you like that, Stupid?!"

Click.

Myeesha switched back over to Tyeesha, now convulsing with tears.

"Some bitch just call my...Some bitch just call my..."

"Myeesha, slow down! What's wrong?!"

"He ate that bitch's pussy! And he gonna kiss me?! And put his lips on the kids?! I'll kill his ass! I'll kill that mothufucka!"

"Hold up Myeesha! Hold up!" Tyeesha screamed. "I'm on my way! Stay right there!"

As Tyeesha raced to her sister's home, Bertha sat in Mari's Beauty Salon office. Mari sat next to Bertha with her arm around her and Pam and Mia sat across from them. The three listened intently as Bertha recounted her brush with Seymour.

"He the same one," she said. "I'll never forget that walk, He bumped right into me when I got off the elevator. I can still feel his evil hands."

Chill bumps covered her sleeveless arms as she spoke of the encounter. Mari ran her soft hand up and down the length of Bertha's arm to relax her nerves.

"You said the Flagship Hotel, Right?" Mia asked.

"Uh-huh."

"Did he remember you?"

"I don't think so, He was moving so fast, He just..."

"You gotta get rid of the Porsche," said Pam.

"Why?"

"Because everybody know it belongs to Miss D."

"She bought it for me," said Bertha

"Just trade it in for something else," Mari said. "I have to find out what's this guy's..."

"That man might know him?" she interjected

"Who?"

"The one Miss D. had invited to the party."

"He's dead too!" Mia said.

"Not Link," said Bertha. "The man I'm talkin' about is only 'bout this tall and..."

"Ain't no man that short," Mia laughed. "That's a Midget!"

"That's his name! That's his name!" shouted Bertha.

"Miss D. knew Midget Molley?!" Pam asked.

"We ran into him at Gino's and Miss D. walked up to him and started talking to him like she knew him."

The Myth of Midget Molley   Ali Rob

"Do you know him Pam?" Mari asked.
"Yeah, I used to mess around with him."
"Can you get uch with him?"
"I can ask his cousin can she get a message to him."
"Who's his cousin?"
"Annie."
"The girl who always come here to get her hair braided?" Mari inquired.
"Yeah, that's her."
"I got her number on file," said Mari.
"I'll call her tomorrow," said Pam. "I have to get home. You staying over Mia?"
"No. I have to meet AJ."
"Where you staying Bertha?"
"I don't know."
"She gonna stay with me," said Mari.
"Okay. I'll call you as soon as I get uch with Midget," said Pam.

It was 11am the next morning when Midget rolled out of the bed. He called Nancy.
"Hello."
"Wassup?"
"You just getting up?" she asked.
"Yeah."
"You gonna do that for me again?"
"Are you dressed?" asked Midget, ignoring the advance.
"I'll meet you at the bus station at 12:30."

"You got your girdle and…"

"You gonna do it?" she asked.

"It's too early for that shit, Nancy!"

"You ain't got to get all crazy, I just asked."

Alene and the others covered their mouths to silence their laughter as they listened to Midget's agitated voice through the speakerphone.

"I see you at the bus station at 12:30." he said.

Midget placed the phone on the hook and headed to the bathroom. The warm water from the shower quickened his skin and washed away his overnight sweat. A smile widened his face as he thought about the two kilos of crack that'd been waiting for him since Friday. He cleaned himself thoroughly and stepped out of the shower.

Midget got to the bus station at 12:25. He walked into the delicatessen and ordered two cheese sandwiches on rye, with mayonnaise, lettuce, tomatoes, garlic and onions, to go.

He walked back out into the main area. Five minutes passed and there was no sign of Nancy. He called her house from one of the many pay-phones lining the wall. Bernadette answered.

"Hello."

"Is Nancy home?"

"Hold on."

There was a long pause but Midget heard a snickering in the background.

"Nancy ain't here Midget."

"Tell Nancy I said get on this fuckin' phone!"
"Hold on."
Another long pause followed with more snickering.
"Hello."
"Who dis?" he asked.
"Arlene."
"Arlene, put Nancy on the phone."
She dropped the phone on the bed and started laughing.
"Midget."
"Who dis?!"
"It's Alene, Nancy ain't..."
"...She ain't going!" Rose hollered out and then slammed the phone in his ear.

Midget snapped.

"I'ma kill that bitch!" he said to himself.

He threw his sandwiches in the trash and walked out on the platform to board the bus to New York alone. A police car slowly cruised by on the Arkansas side of the bus station.

Getting second thoughts, Midget went back inside and called Big Lou collect.

"Hello."
"Yo. I'm tryin' to find somebody to do that; Right?"
"Just come on up, I'll meet you at the Port Authority."
"I can't carry that shit!" Midget shouted.
"No, I got somebody that'll carry it. Just make sure you put her back on the bus once you get it to the

house."

"Okay."

"What time you leavin'?"

"I'll be on the 1 o'clock Greyhound."

"Good," he said. "This way you can head back during the rush hour. The traffic is real heavy around 4 o'clock."

"Okay," said Midget. "I should pull in the Port at 3:30."

Back at the crib, Saladeen and Baseel had thousands of empty vials that they'd copped from the Head Shop in Northfield. They rounded up their little young friends and told them to get ready to hit the blocks. Midget coined his crew the ASO Posse and initiated Tyree and his nephews into a strong organization, willing to go head on with any crew in the city. All they needed was the product.

That problem was solved later that night, when Midget arrived at Baseel's door with Norma, Big Lou's crack carrier. Midget quickly put her back in the taxi and directed the driver to take her to the bus station. He gave Saladeen, Baseel, Raheem, Shareek and Jihad orders to make dimes out of both kilos and to bring every penny back to him. He had a plan and he convinced them to believe in it. Atlantic City wasn't ready for what Midget Molley was about to put down...

EPILOGUE

As word spread across the city of Midget's reentry into the game, he found it harder and harder to move without being barraged by skeezahs and fiends. The crack heads even began showing up at his apartment.

That did it for him. To shield his family, Midget rented a U-haul and moved everything into storage. A week later the condo was ready to move in, but that wasn't enough for him. He wanted his wife and children to be as safe as possible, so he leased a separate Condo. Of course Myeesha didn't understand.

He left out of Atlantic City because of a triple threat: the ever present crack-heads beating down his door, the haters and the cops. To escape the madness, he needed suburban hide-away.

Each time he came to the City, it was on. He moved around town like he owned it. Everyone wanted to be down. He had only one problem, the supply.

He pressed for more kilos, but he could tell Big Lou was on the grind too by his ridiculous prices of Twenty-five thousand a brick.

Midget's flip was so fast that Big Lou could barely keep up. He was only getting four kilos at a time from his connect. So finally he started sending Norma to Atlantic City with all four bricks. That was all Midget needed to raise his game. It was time to put on his show. His nephews had told him about Randy Brown, a young kid from Pitney Village, coming through the block in a black Maxima looking for him. Midget knew Randy was getting his shit from the Dominicans, but he purposely stayed away.

Continuing to connect with Big Lou, he stretched his hustle the projects of BMC Boys and Bacharach.

In Back Maryland, Saladeen and Baseel moved their product like they were operating a produce stand. The rush of business was so wild that they had to move inside Jihad's house, serving the fiends through the kitchen window. It was unbelievable. Midget was jammed up. He couldn't move quickly enough to re-supply the hungry crowds of fiends.

Big Lou tried to meet his rapid demand, but he was helpless. Heroin had always been his thing. Cocaine was new to both him and Midget. But with Seymour lurking, Atlantic City wasn't giving Midget much of learning curve. His supply problem had to be handled and fast if he wanted to take over the town. He was the only one from Atlantic City strong enough to supply the demand and go up against Seymour. But that wouldn't last if he didn't act.

He made a plan. To get his name out, he broke down two kilos into vials, which brought in $100,000 per key. He used the other two kilos, his custom-made Volvo and his flamboyant style to make it seem like he had an endless supply of coke. Soon all the young hustlers knew where to get tons of rocks. Midget was playing the

The Myth of Midget Molley   Ali Rob

game just as his mentor advised. Every three days he'd send his niece, Michelle, to New York in a limousine with $100,000 to pass to Big Lou. The next day, Norma arrived with four keys on consignment.

With each flip, he moved closer and closer to taking over the game. Everyone was taking notice, especially the haters...

On the Strip, Shareek was sitting on the stoop telling Jason how this crack-head Shawna took him to her raggedy apartment in Carver Hall and sucked his swipe just to get him to sell her ten red tops.

"The bitch tried to sell me her daughter for ten more!"

"That's why Tyree said don't sell her shit," said Jason. "She tried to sell the baby to him too."

"What?!"

"Word, peoples! That's..."

"Hi Shareek, Hi Jason," the auburn-haired college student interrupted.

"Daaaam...," they drawled.

It was Nicole Lacosa, the beauty queen everyone called Nikki. She was like that; short and thick, and her hips got her whatever her lips couldn't. On the strength of her beauty dudes looked out for Nikki without asking for any sexual favors. But that was them, not Jason and Shareek. They were shocked to even see her on the Strip. But Midget's red tops were so potent, they brought out vampires at the height of day.

Nikki sat on the stoop spitting mad game to the two excited teenagers.

"Y'all some real niggas and cute too," she said. "If I didn't have a man..."

"Fuck that corny-ass college nigga," said Jason. "You should be with me."

"I'ma good girl," replied Nikki. "But if I were free, I'd wanna be with you, I like your style."

"With Jason?!" Shareek exclaimed as he jumped up. "What about me?!"

"Come here," she said.

She pulled him back onto the steps, wrapping her arm around him.

"You think you can handle me Reek?"

He placed her hand on his crotch.

"What you think?"

Entranced by Nikki's charm, Shareek didn't even notice the black Impala turning right on South Carolina, off Adriatic Avenue.

"That's a lot of man for a boy your age," Nikki continued.

Jason laughed and ran over to a personal customer seated in the backseat of a taxi.

"Where your uncle?" Nikki asked.

"He coolin," said Shareek.

"Where?"

"Why you wanna know?"

He shot a suspicious glance at her. She put his big dark hands on her sandy soft leg. He smiled, showing his little teeth, forgetting all about protecting the whereabouts of his uncle.

"It's a lotta heat comin' from under that skirt."

"If we weren't sitting out here, I'd let you feel just how hot it is."

"Stop playin!"

"I'm not playing," Nikki said, waving some house keys in front of Shareek's gullible eyes. They hypnotized him.

"Where can we go?" he asked breathing rapidly.

"My cousin live in Carver Hall."

"Come on before Jason see us."

They both laughed as they hopped off the steps and turned in the alley. Tyree pulled the car on the Red Klox Bar parking lot and saw Shareek walking with Nikki towards Carver Hall. He blew the horn wildly.

"Hold up," said Shareek to Nikki as he ran over to the bomb.

"Where the joints?!" asked Tyree.

"The gun's by the curb!" said Shareek.

Nikki's eyes met Tyree's from a distance. His expression spoke volumes. As she strutted off, Shareek saw the best pussy he ever laid eyes on get away. He went to chase after her, but Tyree grabbed him by the arm.

"What up?" Shareek asked.

Tyree didn't get a chance to answer. Frantically, he tackled Midget's nephew to the ground behind the car just before Killer Kurtis and Jazzy Jimmy sprayed their twin Mac 10's. Jason ran over to the curb and snatched his gun from the paper bag and raced down the sidewalk on the opposite side of the street dumping every round in the clip in the direction of the two dark-skinned gunmen.

The two Philly boys ran at the sound of another gun. They made it to the black Impala parked at the other end of the alley.

Tyree got up off the ground nodding his head in a retaliatory manner as he watched the familiar car speed away.

...From Gino's Chicken and Waffles, Midget sat back and contemplated his latest successes. He didn't quite believe that only a few short months ago he was flipping burgers for casinos. Now he was served food while gambling at their high-roller tables. In his mind, he knew he was on his way to becoming the Scarface of Atlantic City.

As he continued to eat, he actually started to feel like he'd made it but in that very moment he peered out the window just in time to see Seymour cruise by in his black Saab.

"King pawn to King pawn 4," Midget thought to himself with a sigh. "A long way to go before checkmate..."

The Myth of Midget Molley Ali Rob

COMING SOON!!!

The Ressurection of a Legend

In the next Installment... the rush of the streets...

..."This nigga Seymour's tryin' to see us," said Tyree. "He outta control."

"Fuck all those niggas, We need to kill'em all," said Jason. "Shareek 'a be dead if Tyree hadn't been there."

"Don't worry about those mothafuckas. They walking dead," said Midget. "I'ma kill that nigga! Yo Jason, kill that bitch, Kim."

"Word?!"

"Word is bond. Bang that bitch!"

"What about the product Unc?" Saladeen asked. "How long we have to wait?"

"Yeah Unc," Baseel chimed. "How long?"

"I gotchu," said Midget. "You just do what you do and trust me, I gotta plan, I gotta master plan..."

...and the pain at home...

...Hyleema began crying out of control.

"You don't have to cry Sweetie, Daddy love you," said Midget.

"You can cry all you want," said Myeesha, raising the knife up.

"Come on, stab me Bitch!" growled Midget, walking towards her.

"Move Hyleemah," she shouted, pushing her daughter out of the way. "This mothafucka think I won't kill his black ass!"

Hyleem had just finished giving the 9-1-1 operator the address to their house when the sounds of his baby brother crying, his sister screaming, plates breaking and shoes scuffling ripped through his young heart. He grabbed the gun from under his mother's mattress and ran downstairs. He saw his mom standing in the living room out of breath with blood all over her *"Mommy Love You"* T-shirt. He raced into the kitchen, pointing the gun as he advanced. He entered to find his father stretched out on the floor, bleeding from the neck, in a puddle of his own blood...

The Myth of Midget Molley Ali Rob

NIRO

PRESENTS
FOR THE PEOPLE
-THE SEQUEL-
Featuring:

THE STREET BANGER: "A.C. ANTHEM"
&
THE CLUB HIT: "SHAKE IT!"
PRODUCED BY THE MATRAX &
HOSTED BY DJ FAH D, AK & DJ DO-IT-ALL.

IN STORES NOW

FOR MORE INFORMATION:
609-517-2676 (Beck) -or- 609-665-3253 (Erk)
www.myspace.com/nirothegod

MONOPOLY MUSIC

D-Bear Publications Proudly Supports

BELL CITY ENTERTAINMENT
GET MONEY GANG

PRESENTS

$$MORE MONEY$$: PART 2

IN STORES NOW!!!

...AND COMING SOON!!!

THE EPIDEMIC
BY

MATT MUSE

For more information vist:
www.myspacce.com/mattmusemzmuse

D-Bear Publications Proudly Supports

THE MEMOIRS OF
D-BEAR

By Hakeema Parks

D-Bear Publcations *Coming Soon...*

ORDER FORM

NAME

COMPANY

ADDRESS

CITY   **STATE**   **ZIP**

PHONE   **FAX**

EMAIL

TITLES	PRICE	QTY	TOTAL
1. MYTH OF MIDGET MOLLEY	14.95		
	SUBTOTAL		
	SHIPPING		
	8.625% TAX		
	TOTAL		

SHIPPING CHARGES
GROUND ONE BOOK $4.95
EACH ADDITIONAL BOOK $1.00
PLEASE ALLOW 3-4 WEEKS FOR DELIVERY

Make Checks and Money Orders Out To:
D-BEAR PUBLICATIONS
P.O. BOX 8044
ATLANTIC CITY, 08404

Inmates Receive 30% off book Price When Shipping To Correctional Facility $10.00 PLus Shipping Charges